THE O'MALLEY & SWIFT CRIME
THRILLERS

Corn Dolls

Foxton Girls

We All Fall Down

The House of Secrets

The Uninvited Guest

Deadly Games

THE UNINVITED GUEST

Copyright © 2022 by K.T. Galloway

Published worldwide by A.W.E. Publishing.

This edition published in 2022

Cover design by Kate Smith

Edited by GS & LW

www.ktgallowaybooks.com

THE UNINVITED GUEST

AN O'MALLEY & SWIFT NOVEL

K.T. GALLOWAY

To F&F for bringing some fluffy fun back into our home.

BLURB

Welcome to Paradise Grove, a killer retreat...

Back in Norfolk and back to work, Annie O'Malley and DI Swift are called to an isolated seaside village and the exclusive Paradise Grove Spa.

Renowned for its peace and tranquility, the spa and its staff offer the chance to relax and recuperate in a discrete private setting on its own causeway. So when a dead body turns up in one of the rooms with no clue to who he is or how he got there, suspicion falls on the secretive group of guests.

Cut off by the encroaching tidal swell, O'Malley and Swift find themselves in a race against time to eliminate the suspects before the killer eliminates them.

The fifth instalment in the O'Malley and Swift series that readers are calling 'atmospheric and authentic.

A NOTE FROM KT

Hello,

Thanks so much for picking up book five! Five!! Can you believe it? It's great to be back with my favourite characters, Annie, Swift, Tink, and Page in Norfolk.

With the North Sea as a backdrop in The Uninvited Guest, I did a lot of swimming in it to remind me of just how powerful and brilliant it really is... and how scary it can be at times. I have a lot of respect for the water.

As always, though the county is real, the place names and descriptions are most definitely not.

Without further ado, let's find out about the Uninvited Guest...

PROLOGUE

As far as Nicole Cox could tell, there were two ways to see out her twenties. Drinking herself silly with a little heat stroke to boot, as her boyfriend Ian had done three years ago in Ibiza, or a more relaxed affair with a few close friends and a lot of pampering. Stretching out on a lounger in the spa of Paradise Grove, Nicole was pleased she'd ended up doing the latter.

It wasn't that she didn't like a few rum and cokes and a sweaty dance on a picturesque beach; no, quite the opposite. But it had been years since Nicole had donned a bikini, neon body paint, and little else, and she wasn't quite brave enough to do that anymore, neither physically nor mentally. Nope. Four days at an exclusive resort with her closest friends was exactly what she needed.

Nicole sighed and wriggled her toes, her nails a vibrant orange, painted a few hours ago by a beautician so gentle it had almost brought Nicole to tears. She looked over at the pool, so still it was like glass, the wooden beams of the converted barn reflecting on the surface. Relaxing music played out quietly over hidden speakers, and the gentle clinking of ice in her glass blended together to a soporific melody. Nicole shut her eyes, well aware that she'd have to tear herself away from the relaxing scents of eucalyptus and peppermint soon enough. Plans to join back up with the three friends who were celebrating with her were penned in indelible ink in Olivia Grant-Rose's spreadsheet of activities. Best friend. Professional party planner. Occasional Monroe impersonator. Olivia had been the obvious choice to organise the birthday bash.

Nicole opened her eyes and looked again at the water. Tempting. Cool and invigorating. The poolside was empty, in fact, the whole resort felt quiet. She supposed that was a perk of paying an arm and a leg for the privilege, and going off peak in September. Not that Nicole had paid; the trip was courtesy of Ian, long suffering boyfriend and generous spa benefactor. She wrapped her fluffy white robe tighter around her chest and sipped at her iced tea.

No, she thought. *I'd best not swim and ruin my newly painted toes before I get the chance to show them off.*

Slipping them, instead, into a pair of white cotton sliders, Nicole rose from the lounger and began to make her way back to her room, iced tea still in hand.

Paradise Grove wasn't a big hotel. Instead of

sprawling identikit corridors with patterned carpets, there were winding staircases and neat little wayfairs. Nicole passed through the glass atrium that separated the spa area from the main hotel, and into a dark panelled hallway that led, one way to the reception where they'd checked in that morning, and the other to the staircase to her bedroom. There was nobody about, no sign of staff, or sound of her friends. A clock ticked loudly, echoing around the empty space. A cool wind whipped around her neck, finding the gaps in her gown and making her shiver. Nicole felt her skin prickle in goosebumps and put her iced tea on the windowsill behind her so she could pull her dressing gown tighter.

She cleared her throat, wincing at the sudden noise, and headed to the staircase. Pushing through the heavy fire door to the first floor, Nicole caught a strong whiff of cigarettes. Not the almost sweet smell of newly rolled tobacco, but the acrid scent of something stronger, something that brought with it images of yellowed fingers and rotting teeth. Grimacing, she let go of the heavy door and it swung shut, plunging her into darkness.

Up ahead a door clicked; open or shut, Nicole had no idea, it was too dark to make anything out. Her pulse throbbed in her neck and the relaxation she had felt after three hours of pampering had all but evaporated from her newly tightened pores. Waving an arm around in the air to try and trigger the automatic lights, Nicole swallowed, but her throat was dry and non-cooperative, and she realised she'd left her tea sitting on the

3

windowsill at the bottom of the stairs. She'd have to go back to get it.

Feeling behind her for the handle of the door, Nicole twisted it and pulled. Nothing happened. She twisted it again, tugging harder, but the door wouldn't budge. Her heart was like a caged animal batting against her ribs, her head was swimming. She waited for the lights to turn on, for one of her friends to open their door, for a cleaner to appear with a trolley and the sweet smell of fresh laundry. But the lights stayed out and the corridor remained pitch black.

"Crap," she said, balking at the noise echoing around the silence.

She tried to remember the corridor layout, but it had been a whistle stop tour before her spa treatments started. Just long enough to drop off her bags and change into her swimsuit. She closed her eyes to help her think. There were the stairs she'd just come up at the back of the corridor, and the main stairs at the front. Between them were four rooms, three on one side taken by her friends, and her own larger suite on the other.

Which side is mine? she thought, eyes open, edging slowly forward, her hands out to stop her hitting a wall face first.

The wallpaper under her fingers felt smooth and thick, warm to touch. As her eyes were slowly becoming used to the inky darkness, Nicole could make out the sconces dotted along the walls between the doors. Fat lot of good they were right now. *There must be a power cut or a fault with the sensors.* She edged past a light fitting and felt the paper again under her hands. The rush of blood in her ears was slowing to a gentle pulsing as she edged forward. Nicole frowned, past the quietening in her head she could hear the soft breathing of another person.

In. Out. In. Out.

A whimper escaped her lips, and her hands flew up to cover her mouth. She didn't want to make any noise, to let whoever it was hiding in the darkness know she was there. On alert, her senses now pin prick focussed, Nicole sped up, one hand covering her mouth, the other back on the wall feeling her way. Her fingers caught on the door frame, and she groped around to find the handle, diving in her dressing gown pocket to grab her electric key card. It beeped, flashing green and high-lighting the door in an eerie glow. Pushing the handle down and the door open, Nicole rushed into her suite, tears pricking her eyes, blurring the back of the door as she slammed it closed, locking it shut.

Her suite was warm, bathed in the sunlight flooding through the open curtains. It was soothing after the darkness outside the room. Though it did make Nicole feel a little stupid at how worked up she'd gotten. She knew she was emotional, Ian often told her that, but her reaction out there had been something else. Her shoulders slumped, Nicole walked through the living area, past the squashy sofa and funky looking coffee table with the stacks of magazines she had been looking forward to reading. There were two doors leading from the main room. Nicole took the right hand one to the bathroom and pulled the cord. The fan flew into life, followed by the flickering light, and she walked to the sink and ran the cold tap waiting until it was running through at a temperature that made her skin sting.

She splashed her face and rubbed a cold, wet hand over the back of her neck. Shivering. What if it had been a member of staff in the corridor with her, or one of her friends? She hadn't seen them in a while and now she'd acted like an idiot in front of them. Maybe she would have been better off staying at home for her birthday, the way she had the last couple of years. Lockdown had allowed her the excuse of not having to socialise, and truth be told, she missed it.

Patting her face dry with one of the super fluffy towels looped over the elaborate gold-plated, heated rail, Nicole went to find her phone. She hadn't checked it since she'd left for the spa, and three hours away from it was a long time. It had been low on battery after using it as a sat nav for the drive over from her hometown near Luton, so Nicole had plugged it in and left it to charge. Phones weren't allowed in the spa anyway, though her fingers had twitched near her dressing-gown pocket on more than one occasion. Maybe by the end of the three days, she'd be less attached to her phone. As long as she was still able to message Ian, Nicole was pretty sure she could manage.

On a pretty, round table at the back of the living room, there was a golden tray and some drink making facilities. On the way through to her bedroom and her phone, Nicole placed a long glass mug under the spout on the coffee machine and picked a sweet latte. The pod made a satisfying click and filled the room with a beautiful scent of ground coffee and caramel. Coffee had always been her favourite, and Nicole felt the last of the stress ebb from her limbs with the gurgle of the machine and the delicious aroma of fresh coffee. The little mantel clock chimed for the hour. Just thirty minutes before she had to go and meet the rest of the birthday guests. Time enough for a hot drink and to get changed. She'd brought a couple of dresses and her long-neglected make-up bag with her, relishing the idea of an excuse to get dressed up.

The coffee machine built up speed, spurting hot liquid into the cup. Nicole left it to it and pushed the handle down on the door to her bedroom. She'd been delighted to see the king-sized bed earlier, all to herself too. What a treat. But as she stepped into the room, the subtle scents of sandal wood and rose permeating from the diffusers throughout the suite were extinguished by the harsh smell of smoke that she'd noticed out in the corridor. A quiver of panic rose in Nicole's chest, knocking her sideways like a wave. She reached out a hand, leaning on the wall, trying not to gag at the other smell that leached from the room. Metallic. Sour. The same smell that made her heave whenever Ian wanted her to buy fresh steaks from the butchers in their village.

Breathing through her mouth, she edged into the room, holding the door open with the tips of her fingers. They were all fire doors, designed to swing shut, and

Nicole had already learnt her lesson out in the corridor. Her suitcase was still on the floor, neatly tucked beside her bed, ready to be unpacked properly, her book was on the bedside table, her phone was on top of it, flashing with a beacon of missed messages and calls. And then, on top of her bed, incongruously sprawled across the neatly tucked-in covers, lay a man she'd never met. He was her type, though. He looked tall, the way his muscly calves bent over the side of the bed, even though his broad shoulders were up near the myriad of pillows. His jaw was razor sharp, scattered with dark stubble, his lips a perfect heart, and his hair coiffed. Nicole blinked once, then twice, not quite believing what she was seeing. Sticking upright out of the middle of a very toned chest, straight through what probably started life as a white t-shirt, was the unmistakable handle of a pair of scissors.

Nicole started to scream.

ONE

MONDAY

ANNIE O'MALLEY PUSHED OPEN THE SASH WINDOW IN
her office and stuck her head out into the morning. It
was a bright September, the sun already burning
through the cloud cover, though it was still early. Only
the slight chill in the breeze gave nod to the impending
autumn. The schools were back. Down on the pavement
below her office, Annie watched as gaggles of children
in uniform, bought to be grown into, laughed and
hustled their way to class. Parents anxiously gripped the
hands of the younger ones and fiddled with hair and ties
and laces in the hope of making a good impression.

She whipped her head back inside the bright office
space, leaving the sash up to clear the air of the
previous night's takeaway pizza from Pete's Pizzeria

with whom she shared a building. With the foldaway bed clicked away neatly, and the remnants of Annie's personal life locked away in the cupboards, she made her way to the small kitchenette and flicked on the kettle.

It had been over a year since Annie had seen any clients in her office, so the space was starting to feel more like home, less like a failure that she had to hide away from the probationers she used to counsel there. As a psychotherapist, Annie knew all too well the powers of mind set and self-belief. But she wasn't always known to practice what she preached.

Instead of setting goals with young men newly released from prison (a job she'd done for over ten years), she'd been working with the local police, making up one quarter of their Major Crime Unit, the MCU. Ever since she'd helped unravel the case of a missing toddler, Annie's attention to detail and ability to see beyond the big picture had proved invaluable enough to gain her a permanent place as a consultant to the DI.

She tied her auburn curls up in a ponytail and poured hot water over the coffee, listening to it drip from the filter into her mug. While it brewed, Annie checked through her mental list for the tenth time that morning. Work pass. Check. Notebook. Check. Lunch. Check. Attention span longer than five seconds. Working on it.

It was the first day back in the office since she'd taken a holiday with said DI, Joe Swift, the very man who'd roped her into joining the police even after she'd left before she'd passed probation many years ago to retrain as a psychotherapist. The holiday hadn't been her usual run of the mill sun and sand affair, it had been a mission to find her long lost sister and had ended up with the whole of a small Yorkshire village chasing her and Swift away with pitchforks. She allowed herself a laugh at the insanity of what had happened, safe in the knowledge she was home and dry, and had come away with a phone number scrawled on a piece of paper that belonged to Mim. Now Annie was home again, distracted and impatient for a reply from a sister she hadn't seen in over eighteen years.

Annie gulped down her coffee, after pouring just enough milk into it to stop it burning her throat. She was looking forward to getting back to work and getting her teeth stuck into another case. As much as she liked having her office as more of a home now, it would be nice to have an excuse to get out and back to the station. She found her bag under one of the easy chairs in front of the window and hauled it up to the low table, moving aside the carefully curated candles and an essential oil diffuser she'd bought to pump organic lavender around the room to help her sleep. It hadn't worked. She stroked the leaves of her plant, which were growing in abundance on the windowsill, and spritzed its waxy leaves with the copper can she kept nearby.

Taking a seat, she rummaged around her bag, almost bottomless like Mary Poppins'. She added her mobile, checking again for missed messages or voicemails and trying not to be too disheartened by her empty home screen. There was a packet of breakfast biscuits crumpled at the bottom of the leather tote, Annie picked them out and checked them for damage. They were still edible, mostly biscuit not just broken crumbs. Peeling open the packet, she nibbled on them mindlessly as she packed the rest of the things she'd need for the day and pulled on a pair of three-quarter trousers and a white shirt.

There was a little bathroom on the top floor, toilet and sink in one room that Annie used to have to share with her clients, and a shower cubicle in the adjoining room. She'd been toying with the idea of knocking the joining wall down and making a better space, but as she brushed her teeth and dotted concealer around her eyes, she realised her police career might not be forever and she'd be back working from this space soon enough. Sharing a toilet with clients was one thing, a whole bathroom was something else entirely. No, she'd leave it as it was and keep saving for a deposit on a proper flat instead.

Her phone sounded out from down in the office. Annie wiped her mouth with her towel and skipped back down the narrow stairwell. She clocked the number on the screen, it wasn't Mim, but she wasn't upset by the caller either.

"Swift," she said, turning all the switches off in the kitchenette as she prepared to leave. "Hi, how do?"

DI Joe Swift was a man Annie had a lot of time for. They'd had some rather extreme experiences together since Annie joined his team eighteen months previously, and he'd always come through for her.

"O'Malley," he replied, his voice comfortingly familiar. "Sorry to call so early."

Annie looked at her clock, it wasn't yet eight, but it didn't feel early as she'd been up for hours.

"That's okay," she replied. "I was just getting ready; I'll be heading to the office in five."

"Ah," he said. "That's good. Look, I know it's a bit mean calling you in before your start time on your first day back, and all, but we've got a case that I think you're going to want to be involved in from the get-go."

"Sounds exciting," she replied, leaning over the pot plant, and pulling down the window, sliding the lock across. "I can be there in twenty. Unless you want me to drive, in which case I can be there in five."

Swift laughed softly. "No, no. Enjoy your walk, see you in twenty, and isn't there a Starbucks on your way?"

O'Malley laughed in reply. "The usual?"

"The usual." Swift hung up and Annie slipped on her shoes, grabbed her bag, and headed out into the crisp morning sun.

TWENTY MINUTES LATER, ANNIE BURST INTO THE OPEN plan office to a roar of chatter and the clatter of keyboards. She felt like she'd come home after a long holiday. The sights of her team bent over their bank of desks, the closed door of their new DCI, even the smells of computer fans mixed with station coffee and aftershave was welcoming. Smiling, Annie let the door swing behind her and headed over to the MCU desks where Swift was waving a greeting.

"Annie," DS Belle 'Tink' Lock cried, her eyes grazing the tray of coffees. "So good to see you."

The young DS swung her chair around and jumped up to give Annie a hug. Her white-blond pixie cut was neat around her ears, shorter than the last time Annie had seen her, and her lipstick twice as bright.

"Good to see you too, Tink," she said, hugging her as best she could with a bag, coat, and coffees in her arms. "Tom."

Annie nodded in greeting to the fourth member of their team. DC Tom Page looked like he was just out of school, but he had an analytic brain on him and astonishingly muscley arms that belied his young years.

"Sit, sit." Swift rallied around, taking the tray of coffees, and giving Annie a free arm to pull out her own chair and settle back into the desk opposite his.

He handed out the barista-made drinks to happy noises. The staff coffee machine had a reputation for missing the mark altogether, often spilling out hot water and milk as a gesture. Annie wondered if someone in the building had programmed it to misfire every so often for a laugh.

She stretched out in her chair, her hands lifting towards the Styrofoam ceiling squares with mouldy patches and the strip lighting.

"It's *so* good to be back," she said, smiling. "I've missed this place."

Even though she'd spent her holidays solving a cold case about a missing family and a haunted house, Annie hadn't been back in the office for months. Signed off after a particularly nasty incident where she'd been lucky to escape alive, she'd started to wonder if being in the force was too much of a risk. But now she was back here, those thoughts had flitted away like the steam on her latte.

"You won't be saying that after one day back," Tink joked.

"Nope," Swift agreed. "So, we'd better get down to it before you decide to go back working for the probation team."

"Never going to happen." Annie thought about how much her life had changed for the better since working with the MCU as she caught Swift's blue eyes. "Now, tell me about this case?"

Swift opened his mouth to start talking and was cut off by DCI Robins as she shot out of her office and across the open-plan floor, batting off questions with a flick of her hand until she hit the MCU desks with a poise that Annie admired. If that many people had been gunning for her attention, she'd be so flustered her hair would double in size. Robins' stayed perfectly blow dried and sat neatly on her shoulders.

"Good to have you back, O'Malley," Robins said, holding out a manicured hand. "And if you can possibly help it, try to stay out of mischief with this next case. We can't afford for you to be off again."

Annie's cheeks flamed as she thought of the broken ankle from her second case and the lunatic who tried to woo her then inject her with the plague in the third. It had been a lot to cram in to just over a year.

"Yes, sorry," she said to her feet.

Robins kept a hold of Annie's hand and squeezed her fingers gently before letting go.

"Not because you're not allowed sick leave," she said, grinning. "But because we can't have the DI moping around missing his favourite team member for longer than needs be."

Annie's cheeks flamed even hotter. Swift spun his head around.

"What?" he burst out.

"What?" Robins replied, grinning even harder.

"Favourite?" Tink and Page asked in unison.

Annie laughed and Robins tapped her fingernail on Swift's desk.

"What have we got, then?" she asked.

"Tink," Swift said, nodding at the DS. "Take the floor."

Tink dropped back to her chair and swivelled to her computer, hitting the keyboard, and booting it back to life. There was a picture on the screen, a wide angled shot of the North Norfolk coast, it auto-scrolled to a tall building on a low cliff top, glorious red ivy spreading its fingers up the brick and flintwork. Annie squinted, it looked odd, like a terrace house, tall in stature, only someone had chopped away the properties either side. Instead, an extension at the rear, flashing through on the next photo, housed a glass walkway to an old, converted barn. The next photo showed the house at high tide, the swell of water surrounding it like a moat, and from this angle, Annie could see the cliff was separated from the land, a spit. *Paradise Grove* was written in neat, unobtrusive writing across the very bottom of the page,

"Paradise Grove," Tink said, tucking a strand of white blond hair behind her ear. "Exclusive spa for the rich and famous, apparently. Tucked away on a remote beach in North Norfolk, its only advertising is by word of mouth."

"I thought all the beaches in North Norfolk were for the rich and famous," Annie said, half joking. "Why is this one so special?"

"Waiting for us at Paradise Grove," Tink replied with a raised eyebrow, "there's a dead man, stabbed through the chest with a pair of scissors, no name, no ID, no one knows who he is or where he's come from, and no witnesses."

Swift rubbed his palms together and Annie could feel the familiar apprehension of a new case twisting her stomach into knots.

"Well, what are you waiting for?" Robins asked, already heading back to her office. "Go and book yourselves into Paradise Grove."

TWO

"DID SHE REALLY MEAN IT?" ANNIE ASKED, AS SHE skipped along the corridor to keep up with Swift. "Robins, when she said we should book ourselves in to the spa."

Swift buzzed them out of the building to the car park at the back.

"Don't get any ideas," he said, smiling. "But I don't see why we can't mull over our theories in a hot tub."

"Oh," Annie said. "Only I don't have my costume with me, so maybe we could swing past and pick it up on the way?"

Tink burst out laughing and Annie turned back to see her and Page sharing the joke. She felt like the new girl again.

"Bloody Nora, Swift," she said, elbowing his arm. "Thanks. And you two should know better. Next time you can get your own Starbucks!"

Page's face was puce, but he was gracious, putting

an arm around Annie's shoulders and squeezing her with muscles she didn't think would fit in a regulation police uniform anymore.

"Sorry, O'Malley," he said, before turning his attention to Tink. "Your turn to drive."

Tink waved her keys in return and beeped her Fiat 500 unlocked.

"Tink, Page," Swift said, heading down the steps to the cars. "If you get there before us, I want you to make a list of everyone who is staying at the hotel, everyone who works there, including the ones not there when the incident happened, and tell them all they'll be staying put for as long as it takes."

Tink and Page gave Swift a salute and trotted down the steps to the bright yellow, electric car. Annie led the way to Swift's 4x4 and opened her passenger door, sighing as she sat down. She'd missed the heated seats and soft leather. Swift reversed out of his space and swung them out of the carpark and into the city centre before Tink had even turned over her engine.

"They're not going to get there before us, are they?" Annie laughed, holding onto the roof handle as she remembered how fast he liked to drive.

"They probably will," Swift said, indicating the wrong way if they were headed to the coast. "I wasn't joking about the hot tub and I don't have my swimmers with me either."

Half an hour later, with swimsuits and towels safely stowed in the boot, Annie and Swift were making their way along the dual carriageway to the tip of the North

Norfolk coast. Paradise Grove was situated between coastal towns. Their stretch of beach was private, fenced off at either side to keep out anyone not paying an arm and a leg to stay at the exclusive spa. Annie had never heard of Paradise Grove before this morning, but a quick flick through the shit storm that was Tattle, along with Google, and, surprisingly, Twitter, she'd found a whole lot of hate from the locals. *They've stolen our beach,* rang out a lot on the forums, along with *posh twats* as the most used insult.

"What do you know about Paradise Grove?" Annie asked, as Swift took a slip road off the dual carriageway and swung around the roundabout at the bottom.

He turned down the radio, dampening the poppy beat of some up and coming young band, and shrugged his shoulders.

"Not a lot," he said. "Until this morning, the only time I'd heard it mentioned before was when Sophia was on at me to take her away for a weekend. On a DI's salary, she was having a laugh."

"Ah," Annie replied.

Sophia was Swift's wife, ex-wife really. There was a rumour going around the station that she was missing, and Swift did nothing to quash those rumours though he knew for a fact she was living the life of Riley with a rich farmer named Malcolm. He had told Annie all about it one evening when they were up in Yorkshire, how he'd not wanted to lose face so soon after getting married and had hinted that she had vanished without a trace. But now, years later, he couldn't find a way to come clean, and lived quietly married to a woman who was never coming back. Annie was sworn to secrecy.

"So it's really expensive then?" she asked, remembering how Swift had told her Sophia was all about keeping up with the Joneses.

"Uh-huh," Swift agreed, turning them down a narrow lane banked on either side by a neatly cut hedge, too high to see over. "It's very much word of mouth, *insta-famous*."

He spat the words out like they left a bad taste in his mouth. And before Annie could comment that his whole Range Rover, mansion lifestyle was akin to being insta-famous they turned a corner and were greeted by Paradise Grove itself, and all Annie's words were sucked right out of her mouth at the sight.

It was imposing. Alone on a high spit of land like the last man standing. Not a huge building but striking in other ways. Tall, narrow, the brick facade, dotted occasionally with groups of flint, was awash with blood red as the leaves of the Virginia Creeper began their autumnal change. Even at three stories high, the rampant climber reached all the way to the guttering. The front door was painted a matt black, garish brass fittings gleamed against the dullness of the paint making it look expensive and tasteless in one fowl swoop. To the rear of the Grove was a glass atrium conjoining a large barn with the main house and, beyond that, the sea.

Swift drove the car further up the road towards the building. They bumped over a strip of tarmac which was worn away by years of tidal wash, the sand lay thinly, waiting to be dragged in and out twice a day. Annie felt her stomach drip coldly as she tried to work out when the next high tide was coming, picturing the relentless waves rushing in and taking Swift's car with it. She let out her breath as they passed the dip in the road and started up the gradual incline towards the brass gates of the hotel. As the car approached, Swift wound down his window and Annie could see him searching the side of the road, probably for an intercom or a button to press. But the gates slid open, silently, and admitted them into their folds. He pulled up in front of the Grove and turned off the engine.

Neither Annie nor Swift had said a word since they'd caught sight of the hotel. And, unable to break the silence, punctuated by the rhythmic wash of the waves on the shore beyond, Annie opened her door and slipped down onto gravel the same colour as sand from the tropics. The smell of the North Sea hit her with a pore cleansing, cool slap. She licked her lips, tasting the salty spray that had already clung to her skin. Paradise Grove was giving off weird vibes, a dangerous mixture of money and the kind of thrills that people crave by jumping out of a plane, but she couldn't put her finger on why. Maybe it was the proximity of the water, churning unpredictably out past the low cliff edge, or maybe it was the eerie stillness of everything despite the churning water. There were no birds in the sky, no seagulls screeching for food, or pigeons cooing for their mate. There wasn't even the gentle hum of the bees or flies. It was a vacuum; all life had been sucked away by the bricks of the building or the water at its very edges.

Annie shivered and turned back to Swift, whose gaze was drawn to a window at the very top of Paradise Grove. His face looked waxy and pale.

"Everything alright?" she asked, walking back to him, and looking up to the point his eyes had found. There was nothing there except the ivy and several uniform windows all pitch black against the dropping sun.

"Yeah," Swift replied, shaking his shoulders out. "Just getting the lay of the land."

He turned his attention to Annie, his cheeks starting to come back to life.

"You getting that feeling too?" she asked him. "The whole place is giving me the heebie jeebies."

"Maybe it's you," he said, his eyebrows wrinkled. "Every case you've worked on has been thick with some kind of other worldy... stuff."

From satanic cults to plague doctors, boarding schools to a haunted cottage, Swift wasn't wrong.

"Feel free to drop me back at home anytime you like!" Annie jibed, hoping Swift wouldn't start thinking of her as a bad omen.

Swift rubbed her shoulder. "Not until we've had a chance to check out the facilities, hey?"

He locked his car and started to make his way around to the glass atrium and the spa barn.

"We not using the front door?" Annie asked, walking alongside him.

"Don't want to mess up their paintwork with my sweaty hands," Swift replied, with a short, sharp laugh. "Wouldn't be fair on the 'grammers."

Their feet crunched over the gravel of the driveway as they walked around the side of the hotel. It wasn't a deep building either, just two or three rooms from what Annie could tell by the windows. The atrium loomed ahead, and through the pristine glass, Annie could see Tink's bright yellow car and the flashing of a patrol vehicle in what must be the hotel carpark. There was no way around to greet them. The atrium had no external doors, and the barn it led to was so close to the edge of the cliff that it made Annie's head swim just looking at it.

"That's not relaxing in any way, shape, or form," she said, pointing this health and safety hazard out to Swift. "Imagine getting a back massage one minute and having a swim in the sea the next. No thank you very much."

Swift walked up and around the barn, leaning over the edge of a low fence that made up the perimeter of the grounds.

"It is close to the edge, but it's not *that* far down," he said, stepping back. Annie let out her breath and silently hoped Swift would never do that again. "Come on, we can get in here."

He pulled open a fire door on the side of the converted building and held it open for Annie. Still too close to the drop, Annie scuttled quickly inside in case her legs gave way before she made it.

Contrary to what she'd said only moments earlier, inside the spa was incredibly relaxing. Scented a heady mixture of eucalyptus and peppermint with the gentle tinkle of running water and panpipes, Annie couldn't hear the North Sea at all. The low lights were dimmed enough to create a haven of tranquillity, but bright enough to make out a large pool area, hot tubs, a couple of treatment rooms, swinging chairs, and wicker loungers. It was like something out of a Conde Nast *most exclusive spa retreats* lists. Annie felt a trickle of sweat run down her lower back and rest in the waist band of her trousers. With the temperature set at a balmy heat, she imagined it would be perfect for the swimsuit she'd left in Swift's boot, but less so for her work clothes.

"Phew," she said, flapping the front of her shirt. "Can we move? I feel like I'm already in the sauna standing here."

"It's rather warm, isn't it?" Swift said, looking around for an exit. "But interesting that it's still in use, given the circumstances."

He nodded to the hot tub behind an ornate pillar of faux marble that definitely wasn't one of the original features of the barn. Annie tilted to the side and caught sight of four heads peaking over the top of the matching marble, circular tub. From what Annie could make out through the fug of essential oils being pumped around by the misters, the heads belonged to four women, their hair piled high in top knots.

"Guests," Annie whispered to Swift as they walked

towards a door subtly marked exit. "I suppose the staff will be trying to keep everyone away from the body. Not great for business."

Swift pushed open the door to a bright, and thankfully cool, reception area. From here there were two further doors, one to the glass atrium and the hotel, the other to the carpark. Annie wiped her forehead and retied her own hair back up in a top knot. Humidity and curls were not the best of friends. The space was unmanned, but through the window, Annie could see the unmistakable uniform of a spa worker talking to the equally unmistakable uniform of a police officer in the car park of the hotel. It was an easy conversation, not an interview, Annie could tell by the way the spa worker tilted her head towards the officer, one hand tucked into the lapel of her white outfit, the other playing with a strand of hair.

"Or maybe quite good for business," Swift said, marching to the door out to the carpark and sticking his head out into the sea whipped air. "You, what's your name?"

The officer spun around and straightened up, squaring his shoulders.

"PC Hanley, Sir," he said, half raising his hand in a salute before remembering he didn't need to do that.

"Is the perimeter secure?" Swift shouted.

"Yes, sir," he replied. Annie could see his Adam's apple bobbing frantically. "High fence all around, gate manned, cliff at the back. No one is getting in, sir. Or… or out."

The spa worker tilted her head at that.

"Good, work," Swift shouted. "I'll be the SIO from here on in, all information to go through me."

"Sir," PC Hanley nodded, acutely aware of the beautician watching his every move.

Swift retreated back to the reception, pulling the door closed behind him.

"Two uniforms together are like molten lava," Annie said quietly, smiling as the two young people went back to their flirting.

"Hmm," Swift replied, his eyes twinkling. "Didn't know you coveted a uniform, O'Malley. Right, let's go and see the body."

THREE

Evans, the pathologist, straightened up as Annie and Swift knocked at the guest room door. He beckoned them through the living quarters and into the bedroom, which was on such a grand scale that even Evans looked dwarfed by it, his pink hair clashing with the patterned carpet and the matching curtains. On top of the eiderdown was the body. Annie adjusted her mask and stepped towards it.

"O'Malley, Swift," Evans said, lifting a hand in greeting. "Good to see you both, wish we weren't always meeting under these circumstances."

"You too, Evans," Swift replied. "What have we got?"

Evans turned back to the body. The dead man was half on the bed, his feet propped on the floor, as though he'd been pushed there, or fallen and laid where he landed. His face was pale, unsurprisingly, as most of his blood had leached out around the scissors sticking out of his chest and onto the covers. It looked like a scene from an abattoir.

"Male," Evans began. "Early thirties, well built, obviously took care of himself. I don't want to say for definite, but I'd hazard a guess that death was as a result from exsanguination, probably because of a stab wound to the chest. But I will of course keep you updated when I get all the results back from the lab."

"Can you do me a PM?" Swift asked, walking around the bed.

Evans glanced up at the DI. "They're normally reserved for the dead, Swift, but as you asked so nicely."

Swift raised a brow but didn't take the bait.

"Any ID?" Annie asked.

"Not on his person," Evans replied. "Your officers are checking with the staff and the guests as we speak."

"Identifying marks or tattoos?" Swift asked.

Evans shook his head. "Nothing that I could see from here, but again, I'll let you know." He stood back, peeling his gloves off fingers as thick as tree roots.

"Thanks, Evans," Swift said, taking up the space the coroner had just left, and studying the body.

Evans said his goodbyes and Annie and Swift were alone in the room. Annie walked around, looking at the gargantuan bed, the writing desk and transparent chair. She poked her head back out into the living area of the suite, looking at the squashy sofas and the immaculate cushions. Everything she saw was steeped with quality, marred only temporarily by the back of the uniformed officer guarding the suite door.

"What do you think?" she asked Swift, going back into the bedroom. "Lovers' tiff?"

"Could be," he said, lifting the dead man's hands with his own gloved fingers. "But that'd have to be some tiff, the scissors are in all the way to the hilt."

Annie came closer to the body. The acidic smell of blood was almost pungent enough to overpower the aftershave the man was wearing. Musky and expensive.

"He's very attractive, isn't he?" she said, taking in his angled jaw and muscular arms. "He's got a look of someone famous. I don't mean I recognise him, just that well-presented look that comes with having lots of money. A good haircut, skin care, well-fitting clothes, that kind of thing."

"He's certainly got money," Swift acknowledged, lifting the man's arm to show Annie what he had been looking at. "These watches are a minimum of fifty thousand."

"Pounds?" Annie blurted.

Swift lifted an eyebrow at her. "Yes, pounds! And his t-shirt is couture."

"He must be a guest then." Annie questioned. "Surely."

"Apparently, nobody staying here recognised him," Swift replied, sliding a gloved hand into the man's trouser pockets.

"Maybe one of the guests snuck him in?" Annie asked. "Those four women in the hot tub. Perhaps they couldn't afford another reservation and waited until they were already here. You could hide a person in this room quite easily."

Swift nodded, pulling something out. He held it up, it was a small square silver-foil wrapped condom.

"Perhaps," he said. "Someone definitely knew him more than they're letting on."

"Looks like it," she agreed, stepping over to the bedside table.

There was a phone and a book and a little pot of cream that cost more than Annie's monthly food shop. She picked it up, twisting the lid, and was surprised to find it not full of snake's blood infused lotions, but tiny little pills. They were round, coated in enteric polymers to make them sweet and easy to swallow and to stop them being degraded by stomach acids.

"Joe," Annie said, tilting the pot to show Swift. "Why hide pills?"

"Illegal?" he asked, squinting to see over the giant bed to the pot Annie was holding.

Annie lifted her mask for a second and sniffed at the pot. She shook her head.

"If I was to put money on it," she said, shaking the pot. "I'd say these were contraceptive pills."

She replaced the lid and put the pot back where she found it, tapping a finger on the screen of the phone. It lit up to a locked screen full of messages and missed calls.

"Popular woman," Annie noted, looking at the name

of the sender. "Someone called Ian is trying very hard to get in touch with the owner of this."

"Jealous boyfriend?" Swift asked, looking at the handle of the scissors sticking out of the dead man's chest. "We need to find out who this man is. Come on, let's go and find the owner of this establishment and see what they have to say. We can find Tink and Page on the way too."

They ducked under the tape and out of the suite. Annie pulled off her mask and gloves and threw them in a hazardous waste bag by the waiting officer.

"Thanks," Swift said to the young man as he did the same. "We're done here. Can you get the body bagged up and sent on to Evans, please?"

The officer nodded and clicked his radio into life.

"Lead the way," Swift said to Annie, as he took one last look through the door to the suite. "Nice place to stay, if you can afford it."

Annie left the room and trudged down the corridor towards the main staircase, her mind as heavy as her feet. The reception area of the hotel was as sleek as the spa reception, with muted brass and matt black furnishings. This desk, too, was unmanned, so they made their way around it and up another gloomy corridor where they came upon what looked to be the dining room. Fifties style furniture filled the large space. Teak, curved corners, as much glass on the tables as in the huge window overlooking the carpark and the sea. It was in stark contrast to the modern touches throughout the rest of the hotel; Annie liked this room. A couple of officers milled around, their radios crackling occasionally. Tink and Page were sitting at a large round table with a woman whose face was red and puffy, and another table housed what looked like five staff members, including the spa worker who'd been distracting the officer earlier. Their narrowed eyes all followed the detectives as they crossed the room to join their team.

"O'Malley, Swift," Page said, standing from his chair. 'This is Pamela Parris, proprietor of the hotel. Ms Parris, DI Swift and Annie O'Malley."

Swift nodded a polite greeting. "Ms Parris, hello. Is there somewhere a little quieter we can talk?"

Pamela Parris dabbed at her face with a crumpled tissue, leaving dots of white fluff stuck to her tears.

"My office," she said, her voice catching in her throat.

"Okay, let's go." Swift opened his arms, inviting Pamela to lead the way.

She struggled to her feet, her shoulders hunched. Up close, Annie saw that Pamela's neat chignon was dotted with grey where the dark dye was growing out, the hand gripped tightly around the tissue was marked with age spots and wrinkled. But she could see past the swollen tears to a beauty that age couldn't diminish.

The older woman wound her way back through the dining tables and Swift followed her. Annie stopped briefly to talk to Tink and Page.

"There are only four guests," Tink said quietly. "And six staff, including Ms Parris. None of them are admitting to knowing the deceased. We're going to start with housekeeping." Tink nodded to the other table and the two women in black dresses. "The room wasn't broken into, and they're the ones with the keys and eyes everywhere. Will keep you updated."

"Thanks, guys," Annie said, and she turned and strode after Swift.

PAMELA PARRIS' OFFICE MUST HAVE STARTED LIFE AS A broom cupboard. Found under the stairs, with a sloped ceiling and one small window, sealed tight, too high to see out of. The air felt like it had been trapped here since the hotel was built. Annie pulled at the collar of her shirt again and tiptoed tentatively into the gloom. The desk took up most of the space, at least Annie thought it was a desk, she couldn't see the top of it for loose paperwork and empty mugs. Pamela sat heavily on a rickety old computer chair and dropped her elbows on top of the weekend's local newspaper. Under her tanned arms, Annie caught sight of a black and white photo of an angry man with a placard. Pamela noticed and quickly pulled the paper off the desk and onto the floor behind her.

There was nowhere else to sit, so Annie and Swift huddled together and stayed standing. She felt the heat of his arm through her shirt and the press of the wall against her back.

"I inherited Paradise Grove from my father."

Pamela's vowels were elongated, stretched by the silver spoon she'd been born with. "He ran it as a private members club back in the day when the gardens were over a hundred feet long. He'd have the best summer parties out there. People would be on the waiting list for years because nobody liked to leave. Mostly it was Londoners visiting their weekend homes, though there were a few local men too."

Annie watched the older woman's lip curl, then relax almost immediately.

"What made you change the way Paradise Grove was run?" she asked.

Pamela twisted a piece of tissue between her thumb and forefinger until it had disintegrated into a powdery pile on the desk. She looked up at Annie, her mouth a thin line.

"Women weren't allowed to be members of my father's club." She brushed a piece of hair that had fallen free, out of her eyes and pulled it sharply back behind her ear. "So naturally, women weren't allowed to run one. When my father died, the membership died with him, so I had to think of a way to keep the money coming in."

She scoffed. Annie couldn't work out if it was because the money had dried up, or the very idea of having to make money in the first place.

"And what made you pick an exclusive spa resort?" Swift asked, leaning back against the wall. "Why not a women's only club?"

Pamela lifted a neatly pencilled eyebrow at Swift.

"Have you even been to a spa, DI Swift?" she asked.

"Only with a girlfriend," he replied, his cheeks pinkening.

"Exactly." Pamela dropped her arms from the desk and sat upright, pulling her shoulders back and adjusting her two-piece. "This exclusive spa resort *was* aimed at women. It was the seventies, we were getting more freedom, and I thought a place like this would attract the right kind of people."

"What kind of people are those?" Annie asked, waiting for the deluge of rich and famous names.

"The women who had been banned from the private clubs," Pamela replied with a small smile. "Those women who had spent their entire life being shunned from the very places where big decisions are made and secrets are sworn in. I thought it was time for *us* to have some fun."

Her answer surprised Annie, and the way Pamela's steely blue eyes—now void of tears and worry—dug into her, Annie figured the older woman had guessed it would.

"Look," Pamela went on, "I started Paradise Grove, renamed her from Marlborough Terrace, because I wanted a change, to make a difference. But now look at her."

Pamela waved a neatly manicured hand around her tiny office.

"What's wrong with the Grove?" Swift asked, shifting on his legs and leaning the other way.

"Look at her," Pamela repeated, impatiently. "She's a mess. The sophistication, the grandeur? It's all been swapped out for *bling* and *likes*. It's not what I wanted it to be, but it's what the young people want these days and I still need to make a living."

"The young people can afford to stay, can they?" Annie asked.

"You'd be surprised how many folks these days make their millions before their thirties." Pamela looked beyond Annie and Swift, not really focussing on the room at all. "They're all Tube stars, or whatever the dandy it's called. They want a slice of the Grove, but they'll see, she'll be gone before they know it."

"What do you mean?" Swift asked. "Are you closing?"

Pamela, once again, raised an eyebrow at Swift.

"I don't suppose I'll have a choice after this nasty business. But even if I wanted to stay open, the North Sea has other ideas. She's taking the Grove away from me, brick by brick, stone by stone. I often lie in bed at night and listen to the waves batter against the cliff. And I wonder if now will be the time when I fall with her."

Annie felt a chill sweep up her arms and along her neck. How safe were they if the owner and life-long occupier of Paradise Grove was sure she was about to end up in the sea?

FOUR

"TELL ME ABOUT THE DEAD MAN IN THE SUITE?" SWIFT
said, pushing off the wall and standing upright. His hair
brushed against the sloped ceiling.

Pamela's face hardened.

"I don't know who he is or what he was doing in my
hotel." She sat back in her chair and it creaked loudly
with the shift in movement. "And how he got in is the
biggest mystery of them all."

"The gate," Swift went on. "Does it always open
with movement, or do you keep it locked?"

"Locked."

Annie waited for more of an explanation, but none
was forthcoming.

"So how did we just pass through it today?" she
prompted.

"There's a dead body in my hotel," Pamela replied,
stony faced. "Which means police and ambulance and
god knows who else. I'm not going to man the desk to

let in all the vehicles when I have guests to placate. It's on auto now."

"And you're sure it wasn't yesterday?" Swift probed.

"Are you questioning my ability to run my own hotel?"

"It could have slipped your mind?"

"The gate has only ever been on auto *once* previously, and that was when my late father's funeral was being held."

Annie could see small pink spots appearing on Pamela's cheeks.

"Is there any other way into the hotel?" she asked.

The old woman steepled her fingers and tapped at her lips. Outside a great gust of wind rattled the small window and Annie couldn't tell if the rushing she heard in her ears was her blood pressure or the sea outside.

"There is only one road," Pamela said, eventually, breaking the silence, heavy like a sea mist. "The road you travelled in on. If you take a car either side of that you will end up banked in the sand and eventually dragged out by the tide."

Annie shivered. "How about by foot? I read that the beach is fenced off to keep out unwanted visitors, is the fence low enough to climb?"

"You've been reading those gossip sites, haven't you?" Pamela asked and Annie didn't deny it. "The fences are probably climbable at low tide; I haven't been down there for a while. But even if he had climbed the fence and made his way along the beach, he'd have either had to climb up the cliff to get to the hotel, or walk around to the main gate, which was locked. Besides, did you see any sand on him?"

The old woman was right. There was no sand in the room, and Annie couldn't remember any on the man's shoes.

"So somebody let him in?" Swift asked, his words clipped.

Pamela shrugged her thin shoulders. "It wasn't me."

"And the other question is, why was he here?" Annie asked, her head swam with the warmness of the air in the small office.

"Again," Pamela, lifted her shoulders, "I do not know the answer to that question, though looking at him, one can make a very good guess."

"Were your guests often sneaking people in?" Swift asked, but Pamela's only answer came from the roll of her eyes and the tightness of her lips. Swift took the hint "Well, thank you for your time, Ms Parris. Don't leave the hotel until we say so."

"I've nowhere else to go, Inspector," she said, lowering her chin. "This is my home; it always has been."

Annie couldn't get out of the office fast enough. She sped into the hallway and straight to the front door of Paradise Grove, turning the Yale and pushing out onto the steps down to the main drive. She sat down on the bottom step and gulped in the fresh, sea air. Swift sat down next to her, putting a hand on her knee.

"All okay?" he asked, squeezing it gently.

"Yeah," Annie nodded. "I think I was just getting a bit high off the lingering cleaning products that once lived in Pamela's office."

Swift laughed. "Yep," he agreed. "Definitely started out as a broom cupboard. But why is she using it as her office now, I wonder?"

"Maybe she needs all the other rooms to rent out," Annie pondered. "Paradise Grove may look like an exclusive retreat from the facade but dig a little deeper and I'd say she was running on empty."

Swift got up from the steps and started walking quickly to the edge of the driveway where a tall fence met the gate. Annie got to her feet and followed, the sea air clearing her head faster than a Fisherman's Friend. She caught sight of what had drawn Swift's attention. The flash of a camera lens glinting in the sun gave away a young man trying his best to hide in the bushes that lined the outside perimeter of the fence.

"Get away," Swift yelled. "Go on, bugger off."

The man stumbled backwards, lifting the camera above his head to stop it coming to any damage.

"Dick," he shouted at Swift who had now reached the boundary.

"Police, actually," Swift shouted back. "And you need to get out of here."

"Just doing my job," the man said spikily. "If you'd kept the scene secure I'd not have known what had happened, so thanks for not doing yours."

He threw Swift the bird and stomped away through the bushes and out of sight.

"God," Swift said, coming back over the driveway to Annie. "Do you think it's out on social media already?"

Annie pulled her phone out of her pocket and swiped it open. The screen took her straight back to Twitter and the hashtags she'd been searching on the earlier drive to the hotel. Her stomach dropped and she turned the phone to Swift.

"Bloody hell," Swift said, getting his own phone out and unlocking it.

The Twitter feed of Paradise Grove was awash with internet detectives all with their own theories of how the dead man met his demise. But it wasn't the armchair officers who Annie had issue with, they got those in all their cases, it was the grainy picture doing the rounds. Being retweeted faster than she could keep up with, Annie clicked on one of the tweets and looked in horror at the picture of the dead man lying on the bed. Taken from somewhere out in the corridor, a zoom lens had passed by the living area of the suite and straight through to the bedroom. From the angle, the man's legs were in prominent position, and the scissors stuck proudly up towards the ceiling.

"People are sick," Annie said to Swift, but he was too busy shouting down the phone.

From what Annie could garner, Swift was giving some poor soul back at the station the what for, but she knew that once something got out, especially on social media, it was too late to stop it spreading. Like a contagious disease that the world was all too aware of, gory gossip passed between people like fleas.

Swift ended the call, shaking his head. "How could someone get into the hotel and take that photo if the place is so bloody secure?"

"People will always find a way." There was something about the photo that had Annie's senses fired up, but she couldn't work out quite what it was yet. "Are we trying to stop it circulating?"

"Yeah, fat lot of good that will be, though." Swift was making his way back up the steps, scrolling his phone furiously. "Look at this?" He stopped, holding his phone back for Annie to see. "Hashtag *let's find a killer*. Hashtag *exclusive death retreat*. People are clamouring over themselves to get booked in. What is it about death and destruction that makes people lose their literal minds?"

"Love of the macabre," Annie answered. "Like slowing down when you pass a car crash, it's instinct I suppose. Thought we might have grown out of it as a species, though some could argue we get to see it every day in our job."

Swift puffed out a sigh. "All too true, O'Malley."

A flock of geese took flight from behind the bushes where the photographer had lain, their great white wings flapping loudly almost drowning out their honking. They soared above the fence, over the hotel and down onto the dunes on the far side of the land.

"Maybe the deceased flew in?" Annie muttered as she opened the door back into Paradise Grove.

"I think it's more likely someone opened the gates," Swift replied, with a humourless chuckle. "But let's keep an open mind. Let's also find Tink and Page and an empty room."

They walked in silence back through to the dining room. The door to the car park had been propped open, filtering in the sounds of the steady ebb and flow of the waves past the cliff top. Swift roused the attention of Tink and Page, while Annie stole away, opening a door further back down the hallway and finding an empty games room. It was replete with dark leather sofas and low studded coffee tables. There was a small cards table and a bookshelf busting at the seams with board games stacked precariously on each shelf. Annie tilted her head to see what was available: Monopoly, Game of Life, Sherlock Holmes 221B Baker Street, Scrabble, and rather appropriately, Cluedo. Could it have been Miss Scarlet in the bedroom with the scissors?

The door reopened and the rest of her team burst in, their conversation full throttle, and Annie could make out something about coffee and a bacon sandwich. Her stomach growled and Page nodded knowingly.

"See, Guv," he said. "We're all a bit famished."

"You're at work, Page." Swift sat down on the leader sofa opposite the unlit fireplace. "You bring your own lunch normally, just because we're in a hotel, doesn't mean we can expect to be fed. This is a murder enquiry, not a jolly."

Annie kept her mouth shut about the swimwear waiting patiently for them in Swift's car boot and sat down next to the boss. Tink and Page took the sofa adjacent, putting their paperwork down on the coffee table.

"Right," Swift began, running his hands through his hair. "What do we have?"

Tink grabbed a sheet of paper from her folder and handed it to Swift.

"We have a man with a pair of scissors in his chest," she started to explain. "And from what we have gathered so far, nobody knows who he is."

"Any ID yet?" he asked.

"No." Tink shook her head. "Nothing on the body, and he didn't have anything with him, though officers are searching all the other rooms in case he was a stowaway in one of those."

"No wallet or phone?" Swift asked.

"Not that we've found yet," Tink replied. "Nothing to indicate who he is or where he's come from."

"All the cars in the carpark accounted for?"

"Yep." Tink nodded again.

"Get uniform to check the local roads, see if there are any cars parked where they shouldn't be and keep an eye out for cars that don't move overnight." Swift said to Page who licked the tip of his pencil and scribbled in his little notebook.

"And what about the staff?" he continued, holding up the sheet of paper Tink had passed to him. "Is this the list?"

"Yeah," Tink replied. "As well as the owner, there are two housekeepers, Dina and Gloria, a young man who tends the bar, Spencer, the spa manager, Misti, and the chef, Hans. They were all at work this morning."

"And guests?" Swift asked.

Tink lifted another sheet of paper and handed it over to Swift. Annie could see just a handful of names written on this one.

"Four," Tink replied. "They're staying for a friend's thirtieth birthday treat. Nicole Cox, birthday girl and the one whose room the dead man is in. And her friends, Joy Burrage, Olivia Grant-Rose, and Shelly Took."

"Okay, thanks Tink" Swift put the papers down on his knee and tapped his finger against his lips. "O'Malley, thoughts?"

Annie gathered herself. "We've got three options, well four if you include a random attack which this doesn't feel like. One, it's the locals who are fed up with Paradise Grove. Two, a staff member with a grudge. Three, one of the guests and they're all lying about not knowing the deceased. We've got a hotel that's running out of money and a band of unhappy people living nearby who want their beach access back. I'm not sure if either of those are enough to kill for, but it's a start."

"People have killed for a lot less," Swift added. "Okay, Page, off you go and sort out the uniforms, let me know any reg plates and we can run them through ANPR. Tink, try and get a timeline of where people were at the time of death, which was roughly eleven this morning."

Swift turned to Annie and opened his mouth to

speak when the door bashed open and a young woman came running up, her white fluffy gown swinging open revealing a bright coloured bikini and a very toned stomach.

"Please," she cried, her wide eyes scanning frantically around the room. "You have to help us, it's Nicole. She's missing."

FIVE

ANNIE JUMPED TO HER FEET AND USHERED THE PALE young woman into the games room. She was tiny, a halo of frizzy black curls circling her petite face that made a stark contrast to her chalk-white skin. Pulling her dressing gown tighter around her as she took in the other occupants of the room, the woman darted like a fly from Annie to the sofas and back to Annie.

"Please," she cried. "You have to help. She could be in danger."

Swift had already gotten to his feet and was signalling for Page.

"Hello," he said calmly to the woman. "I'm DI Swift and this is DC Page. He's going to look after you. But can you tell us your name, please?"

The woman's mouth floundered like a fish, her brow wrinkled.

"Joy," she said, blasting the word out as though

speed was of the essence. "Joy Burrage. But that doesn't matter. You need to come and help."

Swift placed a supportive hand on Joy's shoulder. "Can you please tell us exactly where you were when Nicole went missing, and what happened?"

Joy's eyes darted to the door and back to Swift. Annie felt like she'd been caged with a panicked wild animal. But the calmness exuding from the DI filtrated the air and soon Joy's shoulders slumped, and she lurched forwards. Annie grabbed her elbow and guided her to the sofa, not wanting her to face plant the table and lose her front teeth.

"We were all in the spa," Joy said, and took a glass of water gratefully from Tink, who must have slipped away for a moment during the commotion. "We were sitting in the hot tub trying to relax a little after… well, you know, the dead man in Nic's room."

She sipped at the water shakily, holding the glass in both hands like a mouse might hold a lump of cheese. No one else spoke as they waited for Joy to continue.

"She said she had a headache," Joy went on. "And Liv said she had some painkillers, so they both went off to Liv's room to get them. The next thing we know, Liv's racing back to the spa without Nic. She said she'd only been out of her sight for five maybe ten minutes while she nipped to the loo, and when she came out, Nic had gone."

"And when was this?" Swift asked.

"Just now." Joy looked up at him, her bottom lip

trembling. "Liv is beside herself; she can't stop shaking. Please, you have to make sure Nicole is okay."

Swift beckoned to Page.

"DC Page, change of plan," he said. "Can you stay here with Joy while we organise a search? I'll get the rest of the women brought down here by a uniform so they're all together?" He leant his head into the DC and added under his breath, "make sure they all stay together and with you. We may have someone running around the hotel who poses a real and present threat to all involved."

Page's eyes widened but he nodded the affirmative.

"Tink, O'Malley, with me."

Swift wasted no more time. He flew out of the games room and up the corridor back to the dining room. The two women remaining from the birthday trip were hugging each other, their faces red from the spa and the emotion. Swift motioned to the officers in the room and quickly delegated one to take those guests to the games room and stay with DC Page. The staff table had been deserted so Swift ordered another officer to round up all the workers to the games room too. Annie noted that the cups they'd left behind were half full and still warm, but Swift was too busy with the remaining officer for her to mention it immediately.

"You," said Swift to PC Hanley. "Was the place swept when the squad arrived?"

"Yes, sir," the officer replied. "Top to bottom, everyone out first as per protocol."

"Okay," Swift continued. "We need to do another sweep."

He turned to Tink and put a gentle hand on her shoulder. "My gut is telling me Nicole is no longer in Paradise Grove, but can you search the hotel? Take a uniform with you and do it room by room. My hope is she may just be lost somewhere, but the hotel isn't that big, so…"

He didn't finish the sentence. He didn't need to.

"O'Malley, with me." He marched towards the door to the car park and out onto the gravel.

Annie skipped to keep up as the DI strode across the car park and out onto the hotel gardens. He motioned towards the cliff edge and Annie faltered momentarily, reminding herself that there was a woman missing and quite possibly in danger who needed her help. The fence here was waist height, not needing to keep out intruders as the cliff itself did the job well enough. Swift leant over the fence, peering down to the sand below. He waved a finger, beckoning Annie closer.

"Look at this," he said, still leaning precariously over the flimsy barrier. "What do you think?"

Annie thought it was too risky to get any closer, that's what she thought. But at a good three meters away she had no idea what it was Swift was actually referring to. She edged closer, ignoring the cooling feeling as the spray of the sea stroked her face with its touch.

"Wouldn't they have gone out the front?" she asked, still not quite near enough to see.

"That did cross my mind," Swift replied, his voice muffled by the sea. "But we were out the front and then the games room windows look over the driveway. Surely we would have seen if someone had left that way?" He peered back over his shoulder. "If you get just a little closer, you'll see what I mean."

Annie took a deep breath and shuffled to the edge of the gardens, keeping her body behind Swift so if she tripped, he'd at least block her fall. She leant her head around his shoulders and peered over the edge. Where the cliff had been eroded away by the sea water it had formed a shelf about halfway down. Past that, the sand tapered away gently to make a ramp to the beach and the incoming water.

"Oh," Annie said, feeling brave enough to come out from behind Swift and stand next to him instead. "That's not as sheer as I thought it would be."

She took hold of the top of the wooden fence and wobbled it gently. It moved only fractionally, but it felt strong enough under her hands to support the weight of a person climbing over it. The drop to the shelf was a metre at most.

"And look at the way the sand is furrowed," Swift said, his fingers directing Annie to a path of sand that looked newly turned over.

He put one foot up on the bottom rail and swung a leg over the top, avoiding the balusters that were spaced far enough apart to sit between, dropping down to the shelf of sand with ease.

"Right," Annie said, tentatively placing a foot on the bottom rail herself. "Here we go."

She swung herself over the fence onto the narrow patch of grass beyond, then hopped down to the shelf of sand. It gave beneath her feet, only slightly, enough to cushion her landing. She slid down the bank onto the beach and stumbled as her feet hit the hard sand, pitching forwards into Swift.

"Oof," he said, holding a hand out so she could right herself. "Steady there. You okay?"

"Chipper," she replied, smiling. "But only if you tell me that the tide that is gently lapping at my toes is on its way out."

The waves were dampening the sand under their feet, leaving a trail of white bubbles in their wake. The beach stretched widely in both directions, curving outwards from the cove where Paradise Grove was situated. Already, on either side, the waves were crashing against the breakers, blocking their exit to the wider beach. The fence stood tall before the breakers on both sides and they made Annie think back to their conversation with Pamela; the only way the dead man could have gotten into the hotel was to climb the cliff or to walk around to the front gate. She turned back to the bank they'd slid down and her stomach tightened in knots. It was steep from this angle, loose sand trickled down the furrows left by their feet and gathered at her ankles.

"Swift?" Annie prompted for an answer to her question. "It's on its way out isn't it?"

Swift shook his head, his eyes scanning the horizon. "No, it's coming in. But we've got time to go and check out the fences if we take one each."

"But how will we get back to the hotel?" Annie asked, trying to remain calm when all her senses were telling her to scrabble back up the sand bank and on to dry land.

"I think the only way is back the way we came." Swift rubbed at his stubbled chin with his palm. "Unless there's a gap in one of the fences, but even so, the tide is too far in to get across to any of the ramps or steps. You go that way, though, double check for footprints and a way off the beach."

He studied the sand under his feet as another wave lapped at his shoes.

"We might be too late for footprints," Annie said, heading across the beach to the fence separating Paradise Grove land from the public beach and trying not to break into a run.

The sea had never been Annie's favourite place to visit. She loved the water, but she loved it predictable, calm, and preferably translucent. The North Sea offered none of those traits and Annie didn't want to rile it by being complacent. Swift went in the opposite direction, around past the shadows of the spa building to check out the fence on the other side. He shouted something across to her as he went but his words were whipped away by the winds.

The fence was above head height, poked into the cliff face like it was a plasticine model and attached at the other end to the wooden breakers. Salty sea water had rusted the metal hinges and darkened the steel mesh with green lichen. But it was sturdy. Annie gave it the once over, gripping the mesh between her fingers which were now slick with sea spray and shaking. The rattle of metal startled a flock of seagulls who had been resting on the calm waters out past the breaking waves. They took flight, squawking loudly in protest and dropping a shower of water in their wake.

As far as Annie could see, there were no gaps in the fence, no damage large enough for a person to get through, especially one being taken against their will. At a push, someone could climb over, that was doable, but again, not being dragged against their will. She stepped back, looking all the way to where the breakers were disappearing into the water, the fence stood proud above the waves to further out than the tide would go. Turning her head to the cliff, Annie could see a patch at the very foot of the chalky wall that had been dug away. She stepped across the sand towards the cliff, jumping in surprise as a wave caught her unawares and soaked through her trainers.

"Swift," she shouted, waving her arms across the beach towards her boss, but he was facing the other way, and her voice would not carry.

As she got closer to the cliff, the damage became clearer. The faded yellow earth hadn't been worn away by the sea, that much was obvious. It was too focussed, too precise. Annie crouched to get a better view, feeling the damp sand through her trousers and soaking her knee. The hole was about a meter square, dug into the cliff face. The traces of where fingers had dragged out a hole were written in lines across the sand. Annie leant into it, peering her head through the gap where the fence met the cliff. If she breathed in, she could probably squeeze between the fence and the cliff and get to the other side. But there was no way this was dug in the short space of time between Nicole going missing and Annie and Swift getting to the beach.

Annie got to her feet, twisting back to shout for Swift. But as she opened her mouth and turned she inhaled her words with the shock of finding him right behind her.

"Bloody Nora, Joe," Annie said, feeling her heart beating in her neck. "You could have coughed politely or something, let me know you were coming."

"I said your name," Swift said, raising an eyebrow. "You were too busy with your head stuck in the cliff!"

"Look at this," Annie stepped back and nodded at the gap.

"There was nothing my side," Swift said, crouching down to inspect the cliff. "No entry or exit. Just a scary looking cave on the other side of the fence."

He lifted a hand to the fence to steady himself, and Annie saw that the sharp edges had been bent back over themselves, rounding them and taking away the dangers of being accidentally cut when wriggling through the gap.

"I think we've found our escape route," Swift said, hauling his frame back to his feet. "But we can't go that way back, the sea has cut off the ramp. And we need to get moving otherwise we'll get cut off here too."

The sea was already up to the bank where Swift and Annie had dropped to the beach. They waded through the water, lifting their feet high to step over the waves.

"I'm billing you for my shoes," Annie said as her trainers shrunk around her feet with the dampness. "And my therapy."

Swift honked out a laugh.

"You can swim, can't you?" he asked, indicating that she should head up the sandbank first.

"Yes," Annie replied, reaching up and gripping the sand with clawed hands. "But I'd rather not demonstrate how well, right now."

She lifted a foot and tried to pull herself up to the ledge, but the sand slipped between her fingers and away from her foot and gave her no purchase. The waves pulled away, sucking Annie's other foot down into a ready-made quicksand. Her heart raced and she grappled harder at the bank with her hands.

"Come here," Swift said behind her.

She looked over her shoulder to see him crouching with his hands cupped and ready for a lift. Ignoring the voices in her head telling her she was too heavy, Annie put her right foot in Swift hands and felt herself soar upwards. Grabbing at the ledge, she pulled herself up and swung her leg over, landing face first on the sandy ledge and uncaring about her lack of grace, she was up and safe. She closed her eyes and reminded herself how to breathe.

"Er, a little help here?" Swift's voice cut through the thumping of blood in her ears.

Annie peeked out from under her arms to see the DI being thrown forward by a great wave hitting the back of his legs. She swung around and offered him her hands. Taking them gratefully, Swift pulled himself out of the sea and onto the ledge next to Annie. They both lay there for a moment, gathering the strength to sit up and climb back to the Grove when Tink's head popped over the fence and called down to them.

"Pamela says to tell you you're an idiot," she said, directing the insult to Swift. "And you need to come and look at this." She held up her gloved hand, in it was a sealed evidence bag, an envelope visible through the plastic. "It looks like someone has taken Nicole and wants us to know about it."

SIX

We know what you've done and you're
going to pay.

SWIFT PRESSED THE SIDES OF THE EVIDENCE BAG FLAT
to the dining table to read the note through the plastic.

"I'm assuming there was no sign of Nicole in the
hotel?" he asked, handing the evidence bag back to
Tink. "Where was this?"

Annie was trying not to shiver, but she was so cold
she was making the salt and pepper shakers clatter
together as she leant against the table. Her trousers were
soaked to the knees and her hands were red raw. The
tide had been so high when Swift and Annie had
climbed back over the fence, that if they weren't quick,
the sea would block the road out of the hotel, and they'd
all be stranded. Annie snuck a quick look at her watch,
they had thirty minutes before the hotel was cut off
from the rest of North Norfolk. A search team had been

sent to the beach, but their efforts were hindered by the tide too.

"Spencer, the barman gave it to me," Tink said, handing the bag to a uniformed officer to collate for forensics. "Pamela found it in Nicole's room. She thinks it must have been left there as it wasn't posted. There's no stamp or postmark on the envelope."

"Urgh, where was the officer on the door? How did Pamela sneak past him, this whole crime scene is a bloody shambles?" Swift ran his fingers through his hair and blew a stream of air out through pursed lips. "But yes, it must have been delivered by hand. Left there by whoever took Nicole?"

Tink nodded. "That's what I thought too."

"*We know what you've done*?" Annie mused. "Does that mean Nicole has been abducted because she was the one who stabbed the guy in her room?"

Swift shrugged, chewing on his bottom lip. His jeans, too, were soaked through, stuck to his legs like spray on leather, but he seemed to be bearing the cold better than Annie was.

"Tink, can you go and get the three friends from the games room and bring them here," he said, eventually. "I think we need to have a chat with them again about the dead man."

Tink gave a salute and disappeared out of the dining room. Swift pulled out a chair from the table they were standing at and indicated that Annie should sit.

"I'll grab us some hot drinks," he said, scanning the room. "I don't know about you, but I feel like I've brought half the North Sea back in my trousers and it's rather chilly."

He left Annie at the table and headed over to where an urn sat next to a basket of tea and coffee and a stack of small white mugs. The water gurgled as he filled two cups tipping a sachet of coffee and a packet of sugar into each of them. The DI walked like he'd just jumped down from a horse he'd been riding all day, and Annie could almost feel the way the sand was grating against his skin with each step. Her own legs felt like they'd been rubbed down with an electric sander, and she was sitting still. Gratefully taking her drink from Swift, Annie peeled the lid from three tiny milk cartons and tipped them in, wrapping her fingers around the cup to try and defrost them a little.

Her boss pulled out the other chairs around the table, making sure there were enough for everyone. He gathered some fresh water and glasses and added them to the middle, grabbing a few packets of biscuits for good measure. Annie watched him work, silently moving around the room making sure that everyone would be comfortable and looked after. It made her long for the times she'd stayed at his home when she'd broken her ankle, unable to get up the stairs to her flat. She'd been annoyed at the overattentiveness back then, but that was because she had no choice in the matter. What it had shown her, was how thoughtful Swift could be when he wasn't breaking work rules or skirting issues.

"Penny for your thoughts," he said, and Annie

realised she'd been staring at him the whole time he'd been circling the room.

She felt her cheeks heat and reminded herself that he was married, albeit separated and he was her boss. The last thing Swift needed right now was an interloper into the team fawning over him.

"I was just wondering," she said, clearing her throat. "If we're going to be staying at the hotel tonight."

Swift's eyes didn't leave Annie's, his gaze lingered just a fraction longer than it needed to. Annie's insides rolled over like the waves they'd just escaped from.

"Not if we can help it," Swift said, abruptly as they were interrupted by Tink entering the room. He lifted his wrist and dragged his eyes to the watch strapped there.

Tink ushered in the three friends; they sat down heavily at the table and took the drinks offered by Swift. Cradling the cups as though they were made of porcelain and could crack at any moment.

"Are you okay?" Annie asked the woman sitting opposite her, whose bleach blonde hair matched the paleness of her cheeks, a speckled stress rash rising up her neck.

She shook her head, gulping down her drink, her bright blue eyes reflecting the Formica of the tables and blurring to a soft teal. Annie reached out a hand and placed it over the woman's icy knuckles, trying to give a modicum of reassurance, but the woman flinched, pulling her hand away and knocking the empty cup so it rattled angrily on the table.

"Sorry," she said in barely a whisper, righting the cup and pulling a finger absentmindedly through the dregs that had spilled.

"Easily done," Swift said, swooping in with a piece of blue roll and wiping away the tea. "Now, if you'll all excuse the group interview, I need to get as much information as quickly as I can and I thought this would be the best way to do it."

"Interview?" the woman who'd come to ask for assistance, Joy, said, her eyes wide. "Are we under arrest?"

Swift pulled out the last chair and sat down between Tink and Joy.

"Not at all," he said, his voice calm.

Annie knew that, though they weren't being questioned under caution, everything these three women said could provide a clue to what had happened to Nicole, and what had happened to the dead man. Even if what they said was true, and none of them knew who he was, strange men didn't just turn up in hotel bedrooms for no reason.

"What we know so far," Swift went on, all eyes on him now, "is that a man has been stabbed and Nicole has gone missing. There are officers out there right now, scouring the beach and the dunes for your friend, and we are doing all we can to make sure she's okay. What I need from you all, is to fill in the blanks so we can piece together what has happened and we can find Nicole and bring her back safely. Can we start with where you all were when the man was attacked?"

"W…w…we were in here," the blonde woman with the freezing hands said.

"Thank you," Swift turned in his chair to face her. "And your name is?"

The woman took a deep breath, her hands rattling her cup on its saucer, almost tipping it over again.

"Liv," she said. "Um. Olivia Grant-Rose. Nicole and I grew up together, she's my best friend."

Swift nodded kindly.

"Okay, Liv," he said. "Go on."

Her blue eyes grew rounder as she looked at her friends for support.

"Ian, Nic's boyfriend, bought Nic a voucher for a spa treatment as part of her birthday present," she said. "And that was for this morning. So, while Nic was enjoying being pampered we came here for some coffee to wake us up after the drive."

"And did you check in first?" Annie asked, jotting down a rough timeline on her notepad. "Then go to your rooms?"

Olivia nodded. "We're all on the same floor, Nic has the suite and we're all in the rooms opposite. We dropped our bags off first and arranged to meet Nic at lunchtime. We'd booked a champagne lunch and…"

Her doe eyes dropped to the table, her bottom lip trembling.

"It's okay," Swift said, gently. "So you were all in the dining room while Nicole was in the spa?"

He looked around the table at the three women as they held a silent conversation between themselves.

"Yes," Joy said, her words staccato as she answered for them all. "We stayed here for a couple of hours catching up with each other, it's been a while."

"Am I right in thinking you all went to school together?" Annie asked, looking at the three very different looking women.

Joy shook her head, but it was Olivia who answered.

"No," she said. "Nic and I met at school, I am one of the only ones she hasn't been able to shake off. But Joy and Shelly here, they both met Nic at work."

Annie looked around the table. Olivia with her perfect pout and her immaculate hair looked a world away from harassed looking Joy and Shelly who, up until now had barely made a noise. She had the kind of features that would disappear under bright lights, making the quietest of the group look as though she was trying and succeeding to blend into whatever background she was in front of.

"Shelly?" Swift piped up.

"Shelly Took, sir," she said, eyes on the table. "Nice to meet you."

Even in a desperate situation, Shelly was as polite as could be.

"You too, Shelly," Swift replied. "So you and Olivia and Joy stayed in here during Nicole's spa and went to meet her afterwards?"

Shelly's eyes darted across at Joy.

"We went to get changed before the Champagne lunch," Joy interrupted. "Just happened upon Nic in her room as she was doing the same. And it's a bloody good job we did, too. Poor Nic."

"Because that was when she found the dead man in her room?" Swift asked.

Annie saw the way all three of the women sat a little upright, Joy's brow furrowed, and Olivia's probably would have too, but Annie was suspecting she'd had a little bit of work done.

"She didn't just *find* a dead man, DI Swift." Olivia puffed out the words. "Nicole had a severe shock."

Swift held up his hands in defence.

"Of course," he said, nodding remorsefully, batting his dark lashes against his bright eyes. "I didn't mean any offence. I think what would help us most now is if you could all dig deep into your memories and think if you've seen this man before. Could it be someone Nicole has invited here to have some fun with? Is it a man who is known to you? Does Nicole have a history with him?"

Swift nodded at Tink who pulled a folder from a bag hanging on the back of her chair and placed a photograph of the deceased man's face at the centre of the table.

Interesting tactic, Annie thought as she saw the three women reel backwards.

Shelly's hands flew to her mouth and Olivia looked like she was pale enough to pass out. Though the photograph was cropped enough to hide any of the man's injuries, it was clear from his pallor and the way his eyes had no focus, that he was dead. His jaw, speckled with stubble, had lost some of its chisel in death, his forehead not quite so taut. Annie tilted her head to look at him straight on, and despite this, she could tell he was once incredibly attractive.

"We've already told you," Joy spat, pushing the photograph away with trembling hands. "We don't know who he is."

"Take a good look," Swift said, pushing it back to the centre of the table. "A really good look. Because there was a reason this man was in Nicole's room, and in order to find her, we need to know why."

Annie stole a quick glance at her watch. They had just ten minutes left before the team were trapped in the hotel with the staff and guests. Holding up her fingers to indicate this to Swift, he nodded and opened his mouth to wrap things up when Shelly started to talk.

"Nicole wouldn't have invited a man on her birthday trip," she said, quietly, her liquid amber eyes finding Annie's for the first time since she'd sat down. "She's in a relationship and has been for ages. Ever since I've known her, and that's coming up to five years."

Tink was scribbling fast in her notebook and Annie added the dates to her own timeline.

"What is their relationship like?" Annie asked, remembering the missed calls on Nicole's phone. "Nicole and Ian."

"Ian loves her so much, there is no way she would do that to him," Shelly replied, two pink spots appearing on her cheeks. "He's what we all want to find in a man. Doting, caring, he'd do anything for Nic."

From the corner of her eye, Annie saw Olivia raise an eyebrow and scoff quietly.

"Get his name and address and then get out of here," Swift whispered to Page and Tink, before turning back to the three friends. "Try and get some rest. There are officers stationed here overnight, and we promise that we'll keep looking until we find Nicole. Anything you think of, please let an officer know, or call me."

He handed out a business card to each of the women and pushed his chair back to stand. Annie gathered together her notebook and pen and shoved them in her bag. Outside the weather was taking a turn for the worse. A patter of rain knocked against the windows and the sound of the waves grew louder.

"Do you think we'll make it?" Annie asked, skipping to keep up with Swift as he strode down the corridor to the exit.

"Don't let anyone leave," Swift ordered the officer who was manning the front door. "And don't let anyone else in."

The uniformed officer gave Swift a nod and pushed open the door for them. Down on the carpark, as the gravel ended and the road began, the sea was already starting to lap at the edges of the tarmac. Tink and Page pushed past them and ran down the steps to the gravel.

"Don't mind me," Tink called back. "Some of us don't have the luxury of a few extra inches to escape the tide."

"And they make all the difference," Swift shouted after her.

A gust of wind whipped around the side of the hotel, bringing with it a large wave that swept over the tarmac and covered it completely. Annie felt her head swim and windmilled an arm to steady herself.

"You okay?" Swift asked, holding her arm as it thrashed around in the air.

"Just don't fancy getting caught up in that," Annie said, trying to ignore the screaming panic in her head telling her to run through the water and over onto the road. But she knew if she did that, it was already too deep to make it.

"Come on then," Swift said, opening the car and bundling his bag inside. "Let's get going."

Annie wasted no time and was in and buckling her seatbelt before Swift finished talking. He threw a hand over the back of Annie's chair and reversed around to face the road.

The sea was rising, almost quick enough to watch, over the lowest point in the driveway. As Swift put his foot on the pedal and drove through it, Annie could feel the lift of the water even in the heavy 4x4. They shifted on the driveway, listing ever so slowly to the side. The water turning the car fractionally towards the open water. Annie gripped the arms of her chair with her fingers, silently praying to a god she wasn't sure she believed in, as the water lurched and spat them out on the safety of the tarmac.

"Jeez," Swift said, lifting a white knuckled hand

from the wheel and leaving behind a track of wet fingerprints. "That was a little close for comfort."

Annie twisted in her seat, her neck crunching with the movement, and looked back at the hotel. Pamela stood in the doorway, a stern figure in black, her face giving nothing away.

"There are a lot of secrets going on in that place," she said, trying to catch her breath. "Ones that are heavy enough to kill for."

SEVEN

TUESDAY

I<small>AN</small> C<small>OLES</small> <small>ANSWERED THE DOOR EARLY THE NEXT</small> morning with a towel wrapped around his waist, a smile on his handsome face, and little else. He ran a hand through his wet hair, slicking it back before shaking it out, water droplets flew everywhere. Annie was trying and failing to keep her eyes on his face and not let them travel down to the taut six-pack and strong chest. He was like a Love Island winner picked up off the island and dropped down into a detached house in a Luton suburb. Swift seemed oblivious as he held out his badge and introduced them.

"I'm sorry," he said, looking Swift up and down before giving Annie a slow smile that made her blush. "What do you want with me?"

"Can we come in, please?" Swift said, subconsciously taking a step sideways and blocking Annie's view.

"I suppose so," Ian replied, standing back and pulling the door open. "I've got nothing to hide."

Swift walked past and into the hallway. Annie followed, getting a wink and a strong whiff of aftershave. Ian adjusted his towel, wiggling it down slightly, and shut the door behind them, his shoulder brushing Annie's. He led the two officers through an airy hallway and into an immaculate kitchen. A bowl and cup were sitting on a sparkly granite island, ready to be cleared away. A TV built into the bright, azure wall units quietly played the day's news.

"Can I get you a drink?" Ian asked, indicating to the stools around the island as he flicked the switch on the coffee machine.

It gurgled away, mixing the rich smell of coffee with the heady scent of Ian's aftershave. Annie's stomach rolled as she took one of the tall transparent stools and sat down.

"I'll have a coffee if you're offering, thanks," Swift replied, taking the stool next to Annie, who nodded in agreement.

"We have latte, cappuccino, flat white, blonde, espresso." Ian was flicking through the buttons on the machine. "Take your pick."

He swung around and looked at Annie through thick, dark lashes.

"Um, flat latte please," Annie said, flustered.

She caught sight of Swift rolling his eyes beside her as he gave his own order. "Black. And can you go and put some clothes on?"

Ian reached up and grabbed two mugs, putting one of them under the spout of the machine. Annie watched a robin potter about in the large garden beyond the sliding doors at the end of the room. There was no need to focus on Ian's rippling back muscles when the wildlife was equally as beautiful. He excused himself and left Annie and Swift alone in the kitchen, with the hiss of the milk frother and the low hum of the news reader.

Swift gave Annie the side eye.

"What?" she asked.

"Flat latte?" he whispered, stoically. "Anyone would think you've never seen a half-naked man before."

"Jealous?" she whispered back, the corner of her mouth lifting in a smile.

Swift tilted his head, contemplating her question, and Annie felt her stomach tighten.

"Better?" Ian asked, interrupting them as he came back into the room in an expensive looking tracksuit.

He handed Annie her coffee and set to work on Swift's. A few moments later he took a seat opposite the officers with a glass of green looking smoothy and a cold boiled egg.

"Mr Coles," Swift started.

"Please, call me Ian." Ian directed his answer to Annie.

"Ian," said Swift. "Can you please tell us where you were between the hours of nine and four yesterday?"

"Yesterday evening?" Ian said, nonplussed at the question. "Or yesterday daytime?"

"Daytime."

He leant back on the stool, lips pursed, eyes upwards looking at something unseen over Annie's head. "I was at work."

"Can anyone corroborate that?" Swift asked, putting his notebook and pen down on the granite.

Ian nodded. "Three or four people who I share an office with, why?" He leant forwards, his eyebrows drawing together. His throat bobbed as he swallowed in quick succession. The confident, cocky man who'd answered the door was sapping away with the seconds that passed.

"Ian." Swift mirrored the man's position on the stool. "Yesterday morning a man was found dead in Nicole's hotel room. And sometime after that Nicole went missing."

Ian flinched as though he'd been slapped. Annie didn't speak, she sat back a little, watching the man's reactions.

"What do you mean there was a man in Nicole's hotel room?" he spluttered. "Who was he?"

"We were wondering if you might be able to help us with that," said Swift, lifting his bag and drawing out the same photo he'd shown Nicole's friends last night. "Do you recognise this man, at all? Any reason why Nicole would invite someone else to her birthday party?"

Swift was pushing for a reaction from Ian, Annie could tell by the way he worded his questions, but the boyfriend remained slumped on his stool staring at the photo.

"I've never met this man before in my life," he said, looking up at Swift. "Where's Nicole? Does this man have something to do with her disappearance?"

Swift left the photo where it was and took a sip of his now cooled coffee.

"We are doing everything we can to find her, Ian," he said. "Officers worked until dark last night and were back at the scene at first light. We're tracing Nicole's mobile phone and checking her bank to see if there's been any activity on either."

"There's no way there will be," said Ian, wide eyed. "She wouldn't have left of her own accord, not when she's got so much here."

Annie wondered if Ian was talking about himself, or the house they shared.

"What can you tell us about Nicole?" Swift asked.

"She's gorgeous. I'm the luckiest man alive." Ian ran a hand through his hair, mussing up the perfectly teased spikes. "We've been together for just over five years, we met at a drinks event for her dad's company. I was a property newbie, I'd only recently moved away from journalism and set up my own company, so it was a great bag for me. Nicole was working for her dad's company back then, but she's since given that up and is working as admin for an insurance company, much less stressful. Her dad is a stickler for perfection, I guess that's why he's rolling in it.

Nicole had been looking forward to her birthday trip for ages. We planned it together, I even paid for it all. I can't believe it's gone so wrong. Maybe she should have gone to Ibiza after all."

"Can you think of anyone who might wish Nicole harm?" Swift asked, pulling the photo back towards him and tucking it away in his bag. "Anyone who she'd argued with recently?"

Ian shook his head and took a great gulp of the green smoothie.

"No one," he said. "There's no one. She's the loveliest girl you could ever wish to meet. Quiet. Calm. Completely unassuming. Friends with everyone. She goes out of her way to make people feel comfortable and happy. Never had any secrets from me, she was so honest and reliable. I can't think of any reason why someone would take my Nicole."

He shook his head again, his eyes darting between Annie and Swift. In a sudden change of pace, Ian jumped down from the stool and started treading quickly back and forth up and down the large kitchen.

"Is there something I can do?" he said, maniacally. "There must be something I can do?"

"All we ask that you do at the moment," Swift

replied, getting down from his own seat and going to comfort Ian with a gentle hand on his forearm, "is remain here in case anyone gets in touch."

Ian stopped, haloed by the TV screen behind him.

"You think they will?" he asked, curiously detached. "Get in touch? You think they'll ask for a ransom? But we can't afford that... well we probably can, but I don't want to pay money to some sicko who thinks he can fleece us for everything we own."

Annie's mind whirred. Were they rich? Has someone taken Nicole because they knew she could pay?

"Can you think of anyone who might be aware of your financial situation who knew Nicole was going away for the weekend?" Swift asked, obviously thinking the same as Annie, and changing tact.

"Only all our friends," replied Ian, throwing his hands up in the air. "But they could just ask for a loan if they were in trouble. And... well, Nicole doesn't really have that many friends. She tends to keep herself to herself. The ones she does know are away with her right now."

"And you?" Swift flicked his chin up at Ian.

"I've a good few from school and uni days, yeah," Ian replied, pursing his lips. "But that's not possible. It's no one we know, it can't be."

"Even so," Swift added. "It would be good to have a list of people we can contact, please. Names and numbers of Nicole's other friends. And the same for joint friends. And we also need an up to date photo of Nicole."

Ian nodded and slumped off into another room. Annie leaned in to Swift and dropped her voice.

"There were a *lot* of missed calls on Nicole's phone," she whispered. "He'd been trying to get in touch. I wonder why he didn't call the hotel or one of the friends when he couldn't get hold of his girlfriend?"

"Maybe he didn't want to bother her while she was away." Swift got down from his stool and started to walk around the kitchen.

"Then why call her forty times in one morning?"

"Maybe he missed her?"

"You're contradicting yourself." Annie shook her head and slid off her stool too.

There wasn't a speck of dust to be seen or an item out of place. Even the glass fronted wall cupboard displayed crockery to exacting standards.

"Do you have a cleaner?" Annie asked Ian as he reappeared with a piece of headed paper in his hands.

"No, Nicole looks after the house," he said, handing the sheet to Annie. "It's amazing isn't it? I've been here on my own for a matter of hours and already I'm messing the place up."

He nodded to his bowl and cup which had now been joined by the empty smoothie glass. Annie withered inside but drew what she hoped was a comforting smile onto her face. She looked down at the paper he'd handed her. On it was a list of names and mobile numbers. The heading was in a dark blue, square edges, bold, Ian's name written in caps with his job title underneath.

"You're still in the property business, then?" Annie asked, handing Swift the list of contacts.

Ian nodded, he rubbed at his eyes hard with the heels of his hands, reddening the skin around them. He wiped away the tears that followed with his fingertips, licking his lips and sighing at Annie.

"For my sins," he said. "But it's better than working for a newspaper whose ethos I don't believe in. Do you think she'll be okay?"

"Like DI Swift said," Annie replied, taking a contact card from her pocket. "We're doing all we can to find Nicole. Until then, you sit tight and let us know as soon as you hear anything, okay?"

Ian took Annie's proffered card, brushing her fingers with his own, she followed as he led them back through the hallway to the front door.

"Oh wait," Ian said as he unlocked the door. "You wanted a recent photograph, didn't you?"

Though the hallway was large, with the three of them filling it, the space soon felt more cramped. Annie pushed herself back against the wall as Ian pressed past her, a little closer than perhaps was necessary. Swift pulled the front door open and ushered her out into the morning air with a smile that looked painfully drawn on his face.

"Here you go." Ian reappeared in the hallway with a photograph of him and Nicole in a diamanté encrusted frame. "Please take care of it."

"Of course," Swift said, taking the picture. "Thanks again for your time, Ian. We'll send a family liaison officer over today; they'll stay with you while we look for Nicole."

The frame glinted in the sunlight and by the way the gems were cut and from the rainbows that spun around the hallway, Annie would have put money on it that they weren't diamantes after all, but the real thing.

"There's a man in shock," Swift said as he clicked his seatbelt on and started reversing down the driveway.

Ian stood in the doorway, watching them leave. He didn't wipe away the tears tricking down his cheeks, he didn't look like he had it in him to lift his arms.

"You think so?" Annie replied once they were out of eyesight.

"Don't you?" Swift said, glancing quickly in her direction. "You seemed quite taken when he opened the door!"

Swift was right, she had been blindsided by the abs and the low-slung towel, but there was something about Ian Coles that grated on Annie, something that hadn't rung true about their conversation. She gave a non-committal grunt because, for now, she couldn't put her finger on it.

"Do you think you're maybe a little cautious when it comes to good looking men, after your last experience?" Swift clicked the indicator and sped up the slip road and out onto the dual carriageway back to the coast and Paradise Grove.

"It's a good job you're only average then isn't it?" Annie replied, spikily.

Maybe she was being a little cautious, but that was better than being complacent, and Ian Coles had triggered something in her that she was going to pay attention to. Even if it meant a little ridicule from Joe Swift.

EIGHT

The tide was on the way out as Swift pulled up the driveway of Paradise Grove. The car rumbled over the distorted tarmac and pulled up the hill towards the towering building. As they'd made their way across the county, the clouds had encroached and were now threatening to topple over. Annie spotted Tink's yellow car parked at the front of the hotel. She and Page had arrived early to talk to the staff members and collate information with the uniformed officers who had left to search for Nicole as soon as the sun had lifted its head over the horizon, dousing the sea in orange and red.

Swift pulled up behind Tink's car and left the engine running.

"Stay here," he said, getting down from the car and jogging towards the hotel steps.

He was gone less than ten minutes but even in that short space of time, the clouds had saturated, and the rain had started. A steady drizzle at first, pattering lightly on the windshield and trickling down in tiny little rivers. By the time Swift shut the hotel door behind him, it was more of a torrent, blurring his image through the glass like a Kandinsky painting. He threw open the driver's door and climbed in, bringing with him the chill of the September air and the scent of fresh rain. A hint of salty sea followed briefly before he slammed the door shut and shook himself, whether through dampness or cold, Annie didn't know.

He twiddled with a couple of dials on the dashboard and hot air burst through the vents, swapping the rain smell for that of a damp dog.

"Ew," Annie said, winding her window a fraction. "Smells like something has crawled in your heater and died there."

"Thanks!" Swift promptly turned the dials again and the hot air dropped. "It's dog hair. I can't seem to get rid of the smell. Bloody things."

He twisted in his seat to take off his jumper, throwing it to the back of the car and rolling up his shirt sleeves.

"You don't have a dog." Annie put her window back up as the air filtering in was chilly and Swift's forearms were rippling in goose pimples.

"Sophia's," Swift said, a bit too nonchalantly given he was talking about his estranged ex-wife. He put the car in drive and turned around to head away from the hotel.

Annie twisted so quickly to look at him she almost gave herself whiplash. She opened her mouth to ask him a million and one questions, but they all sounded so crass in her head that she shut it again and nodded instead.

They drove on in silence, Radio Two as a gentle background to Annie's overthinking. Swift took a small country lane and ahead over the crest of the hill, Annie could see the sea and a scattering of brick and flint buildings.

"Where are we going?" Annie asked, interrupting Swift as he warbled to Kings of Leon.

"The village of Market Harpleigh," Swift replied. "I thought we could speak to a few locals. The search is still ongoing for Nicole, and Evans won't be starting the autopsy of our dead man until tomorrow. While Tink is looking at the boyfriend's list of names, and Page is talking to the staff, I want to get a fresh pair of eyes and ears on the locals and how they feel about Paradise Grove."

"You think one of them might be involved?" Annie asked.

"It's an avenue." Swift drove through the village, a line of flint and red brick buildings on their right, the pull of the tide on their left.

Little boats bobbed about as the waves drew away from the shore, some of them were already on their sides on the damp sand, waiting patiently for a new tide to lift them. Fishing nets were draped over the edge of a low flint wall that separated the road from the sand banks, laid out to dry perhaps. Though the rain was putting a stop to that. The sight of them pulled at

Annie's stomach, the heavy rope twisted around itself and linked with thick, intricate knots the size of her knuckles. She could tell from looking at them they'd be heavy enough to weigh a person down in the water, even if they could get their arms and legs untangled from the gaps. She shuddered and wished silently that Swift would put the dog-stench heating back up.

The little row of buildings advertised themselves as shops with signs propped outside; a butchers, a bakers, and a post office. What would have once been a bright coastal seaside town looked as faded as the signs themselves. At the edge of the row was a small pub, set slightly back from the road with a carpark at its rear. They pulled off the road and turned into a space. Other than a battered old transit van with more rust than paint, the car park was empty.

Swift turned off the engine and twisted to face Annie. She could see where the stress of the last few hours was etching itself around his eyes. The rays of laughter lines had grown deeper, the pale skin underneath was darker making them look sunken and tired. The sparkle was still there, though, just buried a little deeper.

"I think there's an undercurrent of *something* going on between the locals and the Grove." He rubbed his chin with his palm, scratching over the stubble that had darkened over the morning. "We could see that from the social media posts. I just want to know why there's such a great level of animosity. What's your take on it?"

They doubled back and walked through the same

driveway out of the car park and headed off up the road towards the row of brick buildings. The rain had softened slightly, pattering on Annie's hair and staying there in tiny droplets, too small to break and soak in.

"I wonder if some of the local men used to frequent the Gentleman's Club and they've had their noses put out of joint by the Spa?" Annie asked, not quite believing her own suggestions.

"From fifty years ago?" Swift asked, prodding the exact spot of uncertainty she'd questioned herself.

"Yeah, I know," she replied, stopping at the post office and peering in the window. "Unlikely. Looks shut."

The lights were off and the rain-soaked sky wasn't offering much in the way of illumination through the grubby windows. But through the gloom, Annie could see there were rows of shelves stacked with tins and packets and a small counter with an ubiquitous Post Office sign above.

"Closed over lunchtime." Swift lifted a sign as it flapped from the door.

Annie looked at her watch. "It's nearly four."

"Long lunch," acknowledged Swift. "Let's look further down."

The butcher's door was locked, they finished up at lunchtime. And the bakers only opened until the produce was sold out. From the looks of the build-up of dust and post, that happened a lot longer than a few hours ago.

"Sad," Annie said, perching on the sill of the

butchers next to the standee of a jolly man in a hat and a striped apron. "To think this was probably once a thriving little seaside town."

"Especially sad when you think how rich some of the other towns just like this one are, up and down the North Norfolk coast. What do you think happened?" Swift peered in the window of the building next to the bakery, when the door burst open and an old man ducked under the low lintel and waved his walking stick at the DI.

"What're you playin' at?" he shouted in a thick accent. "Staring in my winda. Get away with ya."

He gave his walking stick another brandish in Swift's direction, wobbling on ankles as thick as tree trunks. Swift lifted a hand in apology and whipped out his badge.

"So sorry to bother you, sir," he said, getting closer to the old man but not close enough for the stick to do any damage. "I'm DI Swift, this is Ms O'Malley, we're looking for some people who know Market Harpleigh well who would be willing to talk to us."

"Not me. I ain't talking to no cops." The man shuffled backwards into his house and slammed the door in Swift's face.

Annie barked out a laugh.

"The old Swift charm works a treat, once again," she said, playfully, and Swift grimaced in her direction.

"Don't mind him," a voice shouted across the road. Annie and Swift both turned to see a younger man in waders and a bright yellow fisherman's hat waving over the low, flint wall in their direction. "He's grumpy with everyone. We think it's his natural demeanour though I'm sure he can be a ray of sunshine, given his name."

Annie raised a questioning eyebrow in his direction.

"His name's Ray," the man lifted his arms in a shrug, showing off bulging biceps with the weight of the fishing baskets in each hand. "I guess that's only funny if you knew that to start with. Sorry."

He put down his baskets and lent on to the wall with both hands.

"DI Swift," Swift said, checking both ways before crossing over to the sea side of the road. "And Ms O'Malley."

Annie noticed that was the second time Swift had referred to her as a Ms and not by her first name. She felt like he was punishing her for something, but she couldn't work out what?

"Hi," she said, giving a small wave. "And you are?"

The man looked about Annie's age with a face tanned with outdoor work and hair bleached by the sun's rays and not a bottle. He had eyes as green as the North Sea rippling the distance behind him, and a certain familiarity about him that Annie couldn't quite place. She felt like they'd met before.

"Kieran Hucklesby," the man said. "My friends call me Kie."

"Mr Hucklesby," said Swift, raising his chin to the man in greeting. "We're investigating a suspicious death up at the hotel on the peninsular. Do you know it?"

"Paradise Grove?" Kie's equally blond eyebrows shot up into his hair.

Annie nodded.

"Yeah, I know it," Kie dropped his gaze to the flint wall, digging into a patch of moss where two large pieces of stone met. "Can't say I'm sorry."

"You're not sorry someone is dead?" Swift asked.

Kie shrugged again. "Well, that wasn't quite what I meant. But I'm not sorry for the hotel. I wish it would fall into the sea already."

"Kie." Annie stepped across the road to join Swift and Kie. She perched on the wall next to where the fisherman was resting his hands. "Can you tell us about the relationship between Paradise Grove and Market Harpleigh?"

Kie's eyes darkened. He pushed back off the wall and brushed his hands together, pieces of moss and grit flying off into the air.

"There is no relationship between Paradise Grove and Market Harpleigh." He turned around to face the sea, leaning back into the wall instead.

"Not an amicable one," Swift said.

"Not *any* kind of relationship." Kie pulled off a glove and started chewing at his thumbnail. "Why would we locals want to have dealings with a woman who couldn't care less about us?"

Annie's phone vibrated in her pocket, but she left it, curious to know why Kie and other Market Harpleigh residents were so annoyed with Pamela Parris.

"Pamela Parris *is* a local, though," she replied. "She

said she inherited Paradise Grove from her father who ran it for years before her."

"A local who never comes into town?" Kie scoffed. "She'd not know the Bird in Hand from the Butchers. She's no more a local than I am Prince William."

Annie glanced a look over at the desolate pub. Pamela Parris wouldn't be the only one who didn't know the Bird in Hand from the butchers given its lack of punters.

"Yeah, you've got too much hair to be Prince William," Swift said, with a sly smile. "How long has the town been in decline for?"

"Since it's been obvious to the tourists that just a ten minute drive up or down the coast is a great sandy beach and all we have here is the harbour," Kie shrugged. "It's all great to look at from a passing window as you speed down the coastal road to somewhere you can build a sandcastle and paddle in the water. You escape the stench of fish doing that too."

"Do the tourists not want to learn about the industry?" Annie asked, genuinely curious.

Kie gave her a look that could skin and gut a fish.

"What?" he spat. "You think people want to stand where you are and watch me sail out with a drift net and a sharp knife? This isn't Cornwall. We've not got the turquoise waters nor the pretty coves they have. No. We're a fishing village that doesn't even have very many fish." He gave an ironic laugh and dragged the baskets from the ground, hooking one over each elbow.

"And besides, it's all too late for that. Now, if you'll excuse me, I need to get these ready for the morning."

He walked away, crunching across the stones towards the boats that were all now lying on their sides on the wet sand. Annie and Swift stood watching for a moment as Kie dragged the baskets on to a boat named *Outerbank,* and started to untangle a section of netting. He was strong, that much was obvious from the way he threw the netting around without a care, but he was quick too, moving between bow and stern in a few strides.

"So they're annoyed at Pamela and Paradise Grove because their village is struggling financially," Swift said, starting back towards the carpark. "But they're not doing much about turning their own fortunes around, are they?"

Annie followed, glancing back at Kie as he worked. Could he have taken Nicole? He certainly had the muscle for it, but why? What would he gain from it except revenge for an age old grudge that had no real basis. She shook her head, pulling her phone from her pocket to see who'd texted her.

"Oh my god, Swift," she cried, stopping in her tracks. "It's Mim. It's my sister. She's messaged me back."

NINE

WEDNESDAY

ANNIE PACED THE CORRIDORS OF THE HOSPITAL mortuary waiting for Swift to turn up. She'd gone over and over in her head the reply Mim had sent. Unable to sleep because she'd been too excited and nervous and happy and fearful all rolled into one sweet bubble of anxiety.

The whole drive back from Market Harpleigh, Annie had been too scared to read Mim's reply, despite the insistence from Swift to see what she'd written. In the end, as he'd dropped her back at her flat, Swift had made Annie promise to get in touch if she felt over-whelmed or in need of a friendly ear. It had only been after a cramped, hot shower and a large glass of Malbec that Annie had the nerve to open her phone and dive in.

And now she really needed someone to dissect the message with. Her best friend, Rose, the receptionist at the station where Annie worked, was away on holiday with a new boyfriend so Annie held back on barraging her with questions. And, though Swift had said Annie should get in touch, she hadn't felt that two in the morning was an appropriate time to do so.

She checked her watch again. Quarter to eight. That was absolutely an appropriate time, given Swift had arranged to meet her here at eight to talk with Evans. Annie dropped into one of the plastic chairs and tried to distract her mind by scrolling through social media. The corridor was empty and one of the overhead strip lights flickered randomly, hurting her eyes. The door to the mortuary and Evans' laboratory was closed tight, and Annie didn't want to venture inside in case she bumped into another being, living or dead, but the flickering light and the lack of sleep were making her head pound. Sighing, Annie stood up and was about to make her way back outside to the small carpark at the side of the mortuary, away from the visiting hours and rammed carpark of the rest of the hospital, when Swift burst through the door with a smile and two take-out coffees.

"Good Morning, O'Malley," he said with a whistle. "Caramel latte for my favourite psychotherapist?"

"Swift," Annie said, smiling and taking her cup. "Good morning to you, too. What puts you in such a happy mood this early on a Monday?"

Swift winked at her. "Oh, you know?"

Annie didn't know but judging by his demeanour

she could take a pretty good guess. What with the return of Sophia and her dogs, Annie didn't want to think too long and hard about it at all.

"I read the message from Mim," she said, instead, changing the subject.

Swift stood motionless, his own coffee poised near his mouth.

"And?" he asked, drawing out the vowel. "Do I need to add a dash of Irish to that?"

He nodded at Annie's coffee, tentatively, his eyebrows creased together.

"Good," Annie nodded. "Yeah, good, thanks. Mim thinks it'd be best if we get together face to face."

Swift's mouth dropped open, his eyes widening.

"Annie," he started, wrapping his arms around her and giving her a big squeeze. "That's not just *good*. That's amazing. When? Where? Where is she living now?"

Annie breathed in the fresh scent of a just-out-the-shower Swift, comforting and citrus. She let herself be embraced, living in the moment of Swift's excitement at her news.

"Oy, oy," Evans' booming voice carried well across the echoing corridor. "I knew it when I saw the pair of you together during our last case."

Annie had been staying with Swift then, and unknowingly dating a would-be killer; they'd not exactly been giving off those kinds of vibes. Swift tensed around Annie's shoulders and then let her go.

"Evans, morning," Swift said, going over to shake the pathologist's hand.

Evans stood a good head above Swift, who was over six foot himself. His pink hair was tied up in a bun at the back of his head and he wore an Hawaiian shirt over a white t-shirt and a pair of cargo shorts.

"I was just telling Joe about a text I've had from my sister, that's all," Annie said, waving her phone around for good measure. "Something going on between us? Very funny, don't be daft. Ha ha."

Swift frowned at her and Annie hoped she'd made it clear enough for Evans, especially if Swift was getting back together with Sophia. More rumours circulating the station were not top of either of their agendas.

"Uh huh," Evans replied, winking at her and pulling out a chain of keys as though he was working a wing of a prison and not a hospital mortuary. "Come on into my office, let's talk shop."

The mortuary was cool, metallic, slightly tangy on the taste buds. The pathologist wasted no time stopping by his computer, walking instead through the plastic curtains that separated the office space from the morgue. He consulted a clip board and then pulled out a drawer from the chamber unit.

"Here we go, then," Evans said. "Let's get our man onto a trolley and I'll show you what we have."

Swift backed away as Evans wheeled over a mortuary trolley and slid the body bag seamlessly onto it from the drawer. He wheeled it over to the work area and switched on the large overhead spotlight. Annie and

Swift grabbed some disposable gloves and aprons and pulled them on.

"So you've already looked at our deceased man?" Swift asked, leaning over the table as Evans unzipped the body bag to reveal a man who had already been stitched up after a post mortem.

Though Annie had sat in on more than a few autopsies now, nothing ever prepared her for the smell of a cadaver. Butcher's shop mixed with a harsh chemical compound. She breathed though her mouth and tried to close off her sense of smell.

"I had a look yesterday," Evans said, peeling back the bag further to reveal the man Annie recognised from the hotel room. "Thought it would be fairly straight forward when I assessed him at Paradise Grove."

The man looked like he was sleeping. His face relaxed, his eyes closed, his lips slightly blue around the edges. There were thick stitches in a v shape from his neck to his sternum, tracking down to his groin. And, now the scissors had been removed, all that was left of the wound was a line of tapered skin on the man's chest.

"And was it?" Swift asked.

"Very," Evans replied, moving the spotlight to illuminate the stab wound. "Death was the result of a sharp object puncturing the upper torso and severing the artery, causing massive exsanguination both internally and externally. The puncture wound matches the scissors that were left in the wound, so we have the murder weapon."

"Were the scissors from the hotel?" Annie asked,

thinking back to the sharps that the fisherman had been using and the hotel kitchen full of sharp items. Was the death a slip of concentration? Was this man taken unawares because he was stealing? Or was he the perpetrator, aggressive towards the killer to the point he was killed in self-defence?

"They looked like a standard pair of scissors, possibly from the hotel, though there's no way of knowing just by looking at them. They're bagged up and with the forensic team," Evans replied, pulling the light down to illuminate the man's abdomen. "I'll let you know if we find anything on it. I've also sent samples to the lab to check for alcohol, drugs, other substances. I'll let you know when we get the results of those, too."

Evans pulled gently at the man's skin with gloved fingers, moving the taut abdomen up and down.

"Ah," he said, eventually. "Here. I have found no identifying marks on this man. No tattoos, no larger birth marks or moles. Nothing. His skin is almost as perfect as his abs. But there is this."

He held a finger on the man's skin and moved back to let the light in. Annie and Swift leant over the body. Highlighted by the spotlight was a small scar line, made more obvious by the all over tan.

"It's a laparoscopic scar line," Evans said. "Probably from a cholecystectomy. You can see the other incision mark a few inches over."

True to his word, there was another identical scar further towards the man's hip bone.

"What's a chole-waddyamacallit, in layman's terms," Annie asked, standing back and looking over the body at Evans.

"It's gall bladder surgery." Evans pulled the two sheets back over the dead man and zipped up the bag. "Fairly common surgery, it won't quickly narrow down our man here with an identity. But we can pull records and see if we have a match for rough age and height, if that will help? I'm assuming you don't yet have a name?"

"Nothing yet, so any help is appreciated, thanks." Swift shook his head, peeling the apron from the front of his jumper and rolling it up with his gloves before chucking the lot in a hazardous waste bin. "No one has come forward claiming to know him from the hotel and no one has reported him missing as far as we know. And now our main suspect is missing too, that is a priority for our staff."

Evans' eyebrows shot up into his pink hair. "The woman whose room he was found in has gone missing. Doesn't that increase her chances of being the main suspect?"

"Not when her friends are saying they think she was abducted," Swift replied. "She just vanished from the hotel with no contact and having taken nothing with her. There was a note too, we think it's from the perp."

Annie felt her brain click into gear, listening from the outside in sometimes gave her a fresh perspective on the turn of events.

"Swift," she said, pulling off her own apron and

gloves. "I think we need to go and have another chat with Pamela and her staff about Nicole and our man here. There's something I need to check."

"Okay," Swift said. "Evans, was there anything else?"

Evans shook his head. "But seeing as we don't have a name for our chap," he added. "I'll record him for the time being as a John Doe. Let me know if this changes."

Annie looked down at the zipped bag on the trolley. He was someone's son, someone must love him, be wondering where he was. But, as of yet, no one had come forward to report him missing. So, whoever John Doe was when he was alive, his family and friends knew he was going to be away for a couple of nights, at least.

The more Annie thought about it, the more she believed John Doe was supposed to be at Paradise Grove. They just needed to work out why.

TEN

THE DRIVE BACK TO THE HOTEL WAS STRAIGHT forward. The traffic was quiet, and the roads clear. But when they made their way up the drive towards the looming hotel, Annie could see the water crashing at the edge of the tarmac.

"We'd better hurry," she said to Swift. "Or we're not going to make it."

"Yep," he said, putting his foot down so hard that Annie felt herself pushed back into her seat. "And the tide is definitely on the way in, too, I had a quick check this morning. Didn't realise it would be in this far already. We'll be trapped for a good few hours, hope you've got nothing pressing to get home for?"

"I should be asking you the same thing," Annie said, her eyebrow raised.

Swift scoffed and drew the 4x4 up in front of Paradise Grove, next to three police vehicles and Tink's car. He turned off the engine and looked over at Annie.

"I'd rather be here," he said, looking right at her.

Annie's stomach swooped out from under her.

"Right." She ran a hand through her hair, pulling it down from the ponytail and ruffling it, just so she had something to do with her hands.

Swift shifted back and opened his door, clambering down onto the gravel.

"Yep," he said, creaking out his back after the drive. "I can't concentrate when there are missing persons unless I'm in where the action is. I feel like I'm not doing my job properly. I promised Joy that we'd do everything we can to find Nicole, and I can't do that at home."

"No," Annie replied, her cheeks flaming. "Right, yeah, of course."

She swung her own door open and stood for a moment's reprieve on the driveway, relishing the cool air on her skin.

"Let's go and find Tink and Page and see what they've got, first." Swift waited at the front of the car for Annie. "Then we'll have a chat with the staff. John Doe got into Paradise Grove and my guess is he didn't climb that fence."

The wind whipped Annie's hair around her face as she turned to look at the tall fence. She remembered the photographer, the glint of lens in the bushes, the photograph of John Doe lying dead on Nicole's bed, and felt her skin crawl with the idea that someone could be watching them now, documenting their every move to showcase on social media only for them to be ridiculed and pulled apart.

Paradise Grove wasn't much warmer inside than it was out. As Annie pushed the door clicked shut behind her, she felt a chill from the empty corridor sweep around her ankles. They walked on past Pamela's office where she sat at her laptop clicking away on the keys, and into the games room on the other side of the corridor. The young Officer Hanley stood in front of the unused fireplace with his thumbs tucked into his uniform. He was watching over Joy, Olivia, and Shelly as they huddled together on the sofa with their eyes firmly fixed on their phones. Undrunk cups of tea and coffee lay on the low table, along with half eaten portions of toast and a plate of muffins and cakes.

"Good morning," Swift said, raising a hand at the women. They looked up at him with pale faces, eyes widening with the terror of knowing Swift could be bringing either good or bad news and at that moment they didn't know which it was. "Nothing to report yet, but I'm going to get an update from my team and will be back to relay what we find out. Have any of you heard from Nicole at all?"

They all shook their heads, deflating like balloons on the sofa.

"We wouldn't though, would we?" Joy said. "Nic doesn't have her phone with her, it was sealed up in her room and she wasn't allowed in to get it."

"Of course," Swift replied.

Annie stepped back out into the corridor, closely followed by Swift.

"They're right," she said as they walked up to the dining room. "I saw it in there, that's how I know Ian had called so many times. But Swift, that's what got me thinking in the morgue, I don't remember seeing it on the evidence list."

"I know," Swift said, quietly. "It wasn't in the bagged up evidence and now it's switched off, I've had a trace run on it already. So my guess is that whoever took Nicole, also took her phone."

"Why would they do that?" Annie asked as Swift held the dining room door open for her.

"Good question. We've got an alert out in case it's switched back on and we've got forensics running a check on her history."

Tink looked up from her table as Annie and Swift entered the room. She was sitting with Page, their tabletop covered in paperwork. Across the room were the five members of staff, huddled in the same way the guests had been around another of the tables. They nursed cans of cola and nibbled on identical looking muffins that the guests had discarded. Annie noticed the younger of the two housemaids staring at her, wide eyed, before dropping her chin and focussing on the peeling laminate of the tabletop. The man sitting next to her gave her arm a squeeze under the table and went back to his drink.

"Tink, Page," Swift said, heading in their direction. "Any news?"

Annie pulled up a chair and leant into the table, not sure how much the other members of the MCU could divulge in such communal surroundings. The staff table was a distance away, but the room was so empty and quiet that she could hear their low voices quite clearly from where she was sitting.

"No sight of Nicole," Tink whispered. "I'm working my way through this list of names, just popped back here to grab some breakfast. Nothing yet. Mostly they're the boyfriend's friends and they don't know a lot about Nicole except for what Ian has told them over the years. She was quiet, good for him, great at baking, that kind of thing. A few of them did refer to Nicole as Ian's wife though, which was weird."

Annie could feel the familiar rumblings of her brain working overtime again. She filed it away with the other questions she had to think about later on and concentrated on Page as he started to talk.

"I've added to the list of staff members Tink drew up on Saturday and spoken to each of them. They have all given their whereabouts for the time of the murder, Dina and Spencer were together, as were Gloria and Hans, Misti was in the spa with Nicole, Pamela was alone in her office," he whispered even quieter, pushing a piece of paper in Swift's direction. Annie tilted her head to read it, it was still a very small list, only a handful of staff. "They're all devastated. Worried they'll lose their jobs. There aren't a lot of options in the area from what I can gather, and it's a close-knit team."

Swift nodded, moving the list so Annie could read it without giving herself a frozen shoulder. It was as Tink had said, two housekeepers, Dina and Gloria, Spencer the barman, Misti the spa worker, and Hans the chef. Pamela's name was written in bold at the top.

"Anyone stand out to you?" Annie asked Page, handing him back the paper.

Page nodded, glancing quickly over at the staff table. "Misti seemed really on edge, she's the one in the white spa scrubs, as did Dina, the younger of the two housemaids."

"We'll start with them," Swift agreed. "And we've been to the nearest town and they're right about the job prospects, it's all very run down. But there are other coastal towns nearby, surely, just a bus ride away?"

"There's something else," Tink added, her eyes sliding over to the staff table. "When Page asked them about the photo leak, they all clammed up. I don't know. Something is up. Right, I need to get back to the spa and make my way through the rest of this list."

"The spa?" Annie asked, as Tink got up from her chair and grabbed another muffin to go.

"The spa office, O'Malley," Tink said, smiling. "Don't worry, I'm not sitting in a steam room opening my pores while I'm on the phone. It was the only quiet space I could find that had good wifi."

Annie laughed quietly. "I was about to offer you a hand."

Tink waved goodbye and headed out the door to the carpark. Page gathered together the sheets of paper on the table and stacked them neatly before sliding them into his satchel.

"Page," Swift said, standing himself. "Can you go and see the co-ordinator of the search and get an update for me, please? Be careful though, you'll have to radio, the road is un-passable, and I think the beach will be inaccessible now the tide is in. We'll meet you in the gardens in a couple of hours."

Page took his satchel and headed out into the corridor. Swift walked across the dining room to the staff table and took out his badge.

"DI Swift and Annie O'Malley," he said, reminding them who he was. "We need to talk to you all individually about what's happened."

"But your officer has just done that," the young man, Spencer, interrupted, his face flushing bright pink. "Why do we have to go through that again?"

"It's standard procedure, I'm afraid," Swift replied. "And we still have a lot of questions left unanswered."

Annie watched as the younger of the housemaids grabbed the man's hand under the table. He rubbed his thumb across her fingers whispering in her ear.

"Are you able to come with us first, please?" Annie asked the young girl, Dina. She shrank even further into herself, ducking down so her body was almost hidden behind Spencer's. "It's okay, you can trust us, and we'll try to be as quick as possible."

She waited by the table, hoping that the girl would extricate herself from her team.

"And can the rest of you head to the games room

until you're called, please?" Swift added, trying to clear the others rather than rely on the youngest member of staff to volunteer to move.

"What do I do?" The young girl whispered.

Misti leaned over the table and grabbed Dina's shaking hands in hers. "Just do what we talked about and you'll be fine."

The rest of the team slowly shuffled out from the table, glancing back at Dina, concern etched on their faces, as Swift pushed the door shut. Annie cracked open a small can of coke and handed it to Dina, sitting opposite her, hoping to fill her cheeks with more colour as she was looking on the verge of keeling over.

"Our priority is to make sure you're all okay and can go home soon," Annie said as Swift sat down next to her. "It can't be nice being away from your family for so long when you're not normally expected to stay overnight?"

She left space for Dina to answer. The young girl looked in her teens, the black dress and white pinny swamped her tiny frame. Her skin was flawless, her thick hair pulled back in a ponytail. Her feet were tucked under her chair, her arms wrapped around her chest as she tried to take up as little space as possible. Under Dina's chair, Annie could see battered plimsoles, the kind she used to wear for PE that cost pennies from the supermarkets. Dina's feet looked red raw around them, the rubber soles thin and worn.

"We've all been staying on the top floor," she whispered into her chest. "It wasn't too bad. At least Spencer was with me. But I do miss my cat."

"What is the deal with you and Spencer?" Swift asked, taking a can of coke for himself.

Dina looked at Swift with wide eyes.

"We're together," she said. "Like boyfriend and girl-friend together. But you can't tell Pamela as it's not allowed, and we might get asked to leave. I wasn't supposed to tell you that, he told me to keep it a secret from you too. Please don't say anything."

Tears spilled from her eyes and tracked down her face to her lips. She caught them with her tongue, her hands wrapped tightly around the drinks can.

"If there's no reason to tell Pamela then we certainly won't, will we Swift?" Annie asked him pointedly.

"No." He shook his head. "Of course not. That's your private business."

Dina hurriedly wiped her cheeks with the sleeve of her dress.

"Thank you," she added.

"So you were all at work on Monday when the group of guests arrived," Annie began. "Is it normal that there's only one group of guests at the Grove at any one time?"

Dina shook her head. "Not really, but it's the end of peak season and there's normally a changeover in September from the rich mums and their kids, to the childless groups of women. The very beginning of September is often quiet."

"Where were you on Saturday morning?" Annie added.

Dina looked down at her fingers, picking away at the skin on her thumb until a petal of red blossomed across the skin. When she looked up at Annie again, her pupils had dilated so rapidly her once blue eyes were as dark as the rain clouds covering the sky.

"I can't afford to lose my job," she said, still picking unconsciously at her thumb. "Spencer and I are going to get a place together, we've both been saving up to be able to get away…"

She stopped talking, her eyes darting between Annie and Swift.

"What makes you think you're going to lose your job?" Annie asked. "It's not just your relationship with Spencer, is it?"

Dina's lip began to wobble, and she sniffed heavily.

"No," she said in barely a whisper. "It was me, I did it."

Annie balked. Was this young girl admitting to stabbing their John Doe?

"What did you do, Dina?" she asked, glancing sideways to Swift whose hand was hovering over his mobile phone.

"I… I let the dead man into the hotel," Dina said, breaking down and bursting into tears. "It's my fault he's dead, and now I'm going to lose my job and I'll probably lose Spencer and I'll have to stay at home forever. And I can't do that."

ELEVEN

Swift sat forward in his chair and placed a gentle hand on Dina's. Annie saw the young girl flinch, eyeing the DI warily, her whole body looked tense and ready to flee. And then her shoulders slumped and her hands relaxed, the energy sapped right out of her like a marionette with its strings cut. Annie had seen that kind of reaction before in children who were always on edge, waiting for the next slap or push, or overenthusiastic nudge. Her heart went out to Dina; there must be a reason she so desperately wanted to keep her job, and Annie guessed escaping from home might have a lot to do with it.

"Can you tell us what happened?" Swift asked, gently. "Take your time but try to remember as much detail as you can."

Dina took a deep breath and squared her shoulders, drawing her hands out from under Swift's and taking a long swig of her drink.

"My morning jobs on changeover days tend to be to get the rooms ready. I strip the beds and bag up the laundry, I hoover the mattress, remake the bed. Bleach the bathrooms. That kind of thing. I've been doing it for such a long time now—I started when I was doing my GCSEs as a weekend cleaner—that it's almost autopilot. To be honest, I quite enjoy that bit, no guests, no one moaning at me. I can put my music on and just get on with things."

Dina chewed the inside of her cheek, drawing the corner of her lip into her mouth. Neither Annie nor Swift said a word, they waited patiently for Dina to continue, and after a moment, she did.

"Saturday was no different." Dina popped her lips, playing for time, maybe trying to figure out how to wrap them around the words she wanted to say. "Except... when I went to take out the rubbish to the bins at the back of the carpark, I saw someone on the other side of the fence."

"Our John Doe?" Swift asked.

Dina nodded. "Yeah. He was waving at me to get my attention, like he'd been waiting there for ages rather than just ringing the bell on the gate. I should have realised then. Anyway. I threw out the rubbish and went to see what he wanted. I don't know if you've been round there, but the fence is high, and he must have walked through quite a lot of bushes to get to it."

Annie nodded; the perimeter fence was impenetrable on all sides except the beach side.

"He was really fit," Dina continued. "Like, proper

gorgeous. Don't tell Spencer I said that, though, will you? And he looked rich, like, his suit was clean, and he just had that air about him, you know? When I asked him what he was doing he smiled at me and called me in closer, like he wanted to share a secret with me. And I was happy to listen. Stupid girl." Dina shook her head. "Won over by a proper gorgeous face."

"What did he say?" Swift asked. "And did he have any accent? Local. Northern. Anything at all you can remember?"

"He sounded like someone in a movie, like, those old movies with heroes and heroines. Jane Austen or Sherlock Holmes. I think he was posh. And he told me if I let him in the gate with no one knowing then he'd give me some money." Dina dropped her eyes to the table, her bottom lip quivering. "I couldn't turn down free money, not five hundred pounds, no way. But I wish I had; I wish I'd told him to go away. Then he'd not be dead, and that woman might not be missing."

"So you think the two are connected?" Annie asked.

Dina looked at her like she had two heads. "Well yeah, don't you?"

"It's a possibility we're looking in to," Swift replied. "Can you tell us why *you* think they are?"

"Well, apart from him being found dead in her bedroom," Dina said, looking at them both incredulously. "He said to me at the gate, when I was letting him into the hotel, he was a surprise for the birthday girl."

Annie looked over at Swift who gave her a nod.

"Thank you so much, Dina," Annie said, sitting back on her chair. "I'll walk you through to the games room now. We'll speak to Spencer next, but don't worry, we can protect you if you need it."

"I don't need protecting from Spencer," Dina replied, a little too quickly. "Just don't tell him I said the dead guy was fit, yeah?"

The two women stood up and Annie put a hand on Dina's shoulder.

"You know you're not to blame for his death?" she said, kindly. "He used you to gain access to the hotel, nothing more."

Dina nodded, but Annie could tell she didn't believe the words.

"Dina," Swift called out as Annie was pulling the door open for them to leave. "Do you know anything about the note that was left after Nicole was taken?"

Dina shook her head quickly from side to side, eyes on the floor. "Sorry," she said, scampering out the dining room and down the corridor to the games room.

Olivia, Joy, and Shelley were still huddled together, as though they were stuck in a limbo, waiting for their friend's return. Misti was scrolling on her phone, lounging on a chaise at the back of the room. Gloria and Hans had a pack of cards out, quietly knocking on the coffee table in a game of Gin Rummy.

"Where's Spencer?" Annie quietly asked the officer, as Dina perched with Misti on the end of the chaise.

"He said he needed the bathroom," Officer Hanley replied. "I'll send him through when he's back."

Annie nodded at Hanley, glancing over the room as she left; Misti's face was set in stone as Dina gave an almost imperceptible shake of her head. Annie made her way back to the dining room, her mind whirring with what Dina had just told them. So the dead man was known to Nicole. He told Dina he was a birthday surprise, if he didn't know Nicole then how would he have known it was her birthday? And why would a random visit from a stranger be a happy surprise?

She mulled all the questions over as she walked to the back of the hotel. Passing by Pamela's office Annie heard a voice, so low she almost missed it. The door was open a crack, so Annie tiptoed past the opening and stopped, holding her breath as she listened.

"You promised me," the hotel owner hissed. "You can't say a word. Not yet. They'll kill me."

Annie frowned, trying and failing to hear the voice on the other end of the receiver. Who was Pamela talking to? The silence stretched out and Annie was about to leave when Pamela swore loudly and slammed the phone down with a crash. Annie heard a chair scrape across the floor and she scurried away, pushing through the door to the dining room, her neck tingling with the fear of Pamela coming out of her office and seeing her eavesdropping.

"You okay?" Swift asked, as she shivered her way back to the table.

Annie sat back down, checking over her shoulder to make sure Pamela hadn't followed her, and relayed to Swift what she had heard.

"Can't say a word about what, I wonder?" Swift mused. "Who is she so afraid of?"

"I don't know," said Annie. "But do you think we should call her in here to talk to again?"

Swift put his elbows on the table and steepled his fingers.

"Let's wait and see what she does," he said. "I'll get Page to keep a close eye on her."

He lifted his phone from the table and swiped to find DC Page in his contacts. Annie left him to it, walking to the door to the carpark. She turned the handle and slipped out into the drizzle. The sound of the sea smothered her ears, drowning out all of the seagulls and the police chatter. It even softened her thoughts as it crashed against the cliff at the end of the garden. Annie couldn't focus on anything other than the rush of water. She crunched over the gravel to the fence, picturing John Doe on the other side of it, flashing a grin and knowing he'd get what he wanted. The fence towered over her, tilted outwards at the top to stop people climbing in. It had felt a bit ominous when Annie had seen it when they'd first arrived. Now, after overhearing Pamela's conversation, the dead man, and the missing woman, the fence felt like a prison boundary.

Annie walked along its perimeter, all the way down to the gardens at the back. The spa building was lit up from the inside, and Annie could see Tink's bright blond hair through one of the windows. She turned inwards and made her way across the grass to the edge of the cliff where she and Swift had climbed down yesterday. Peering over the smaller fence here, Annie felt a wave of dizziness as she saw the sea below. Her whole body lurched forwards, and for a split second, Annie imagined herself pitching over the edge and into the churning waves below. There would be no escape. The water was deep there now, unpredictable in its movement. White frothy waves hit the cliff, spraying up the sand bank and hitting the corner of the spa barn with such ferocity, Annie was sure it would be swept out with each tumble. The wind whipped across Annie's face, salty and cool with sea water, bringing her back to the present and away from the edge of the cliff.

"You okay, there?" Swift had come up behind Annie and was standing next to her. Annie nodded, not quite able to swallow the clod of fear that was choking her throat and blocking her words. "I've told Page not to meet us here anymore, it's a bit choppy out for a start. He's going to keep a close eye on Pamela and see us tomorrow at the station instead."

Annie nodded again.

Swift laughed, not unkindly. "Shall we get in and finish talking to the rest of the team? My guess is Spencer might have a few things to say, given that he and Dina are each other's alibis, let's hope he's reappeared."

"Sure," Annie replied, taking a deep breath, her words returning. "We also need to reinterview the friends, given that our John Doe was known to Nicole. Do you think she could keep an affair secret if she was planning on inviting him to her birthday getaway?"

"She didn't invite him, though," Swift reminded Annie. "He said he was a surprise. Maybe he was fed up of being a secret."

They started to walk back to the dining room when Annie looked behind her.

"Maybe," Annie agreed. "And do you think we should get Tink in from the spa? It looks like it's about to float out to sea."

Swift glanced back over his own shoulder and tilted his head in thought. "I think she'll be okay for another fifty years or so." He winked at Annie and headed inside.

Annie stood for a moment of stillness in the rain and wind that gusted around her, she looked at the water as it reached its fingers up the side of the cliff and caressed the edge of the barn.

Fifty years? she thought, shaking her head. There was little chance of that barn seeing out the end of the year, let alone another forty-nine of them. The sea was coming to take the barn and there was nothing anyone could do about it. Goosebumps prickled out over her body; fingers of dread tickled up into her scalp. Annie shivered and ran back inside to the warmth of the hotel to wait for the tide to ebb so she could go home.

TWELVE

THURSDAY

ANNIE AWOKE THE NEXT MORNING WITH THE TASTE OF the sea still on her lips. She showered quickly and pulled on some trousers and a jumper, grabbing spoonfuls of cereal as she moved around her tiny office-cum-flat. They'd stayed late at Paradise Grove, talking to all the staff, and then again to the friends of Nicole, waiting for the tide to recede. The search party had returned empty handed. There had been no sign of Nicole anywhere along the coast, and they'd searched down to Market Harpleigh and up to the village in the other direction, too. This morning they would be moving inland, but Annie could tell in the leading officer's voice that, as the hours passed, so did their chances of finding Nicole alive, or finding her at all.

Annie had popped into Pete's Pizza after Swift had dropped her at the door, Swift himself had cried off stopping with excuses to get home. She'd ordered a large, deep-pan veggie pizza with extra mushrooms and divulged as much as she could to Pete across the counter as he'd made her dinner from scratch. Pushing open the window to let out the smell of last night's dinner, consumed on her little camp bed watching reruns of Schitt's Creek, sounds from the street below filtered into her flat as the day started with the deliveries to the businesses that lined the cobbled street below. Annie knew that she should move, ideally into a proper flat, and not one patched together from scraps of a now unused office space. But Annie loved her flat, it was hers, and she loved having Pete the pizza man downstairs, and being in the centre of the city. Her mum had told her, the last time they spoke, that she wasn't doing herself any favours in the romance department living in an office, but Annie wasn't in any hurry to repeat her failed attempts at a love life.

With that in mind, Annie glugged the last of her tea, hoping to quash some of the guilt of not having spoken to her mum in months. They'd only talked once since Annie had returned home from the Yorkshire Dales with Swift, and not at all since getting in touch with Mim. There was a time and a place to tell her mum that she was back in contact with her little sister, and over text was not it.

The sun was out as Annie locked her front door and headed off down the cobbled street to the police station.

It was only a short walk, but Annie often used the time to figure out the plot of her latest case out in her head. This morning she was trying to work out the logistics of someone abducting Nicole in the time between her finding the dead man, and the police arriving. There was a certain amount of cockiness in the abduction, a confidence that, whoever it was who took Nicole, could do so unseen by the arriving police and her friends, not to mention the staff who were always present. It would also take a great amount of planning. They would have needed to know the hotel layout, and they would have needed to know who their target was.

Annie was chewing over the idea of getting a list of previous guests as she walked up the steps to the station and through the doors.

"Alright, stranger," Rose said from the reception desk.

She looked luminous; tanned and glowing after a holiday that, from Rose's beaming smile, Annie guessed had gone well.

"Rose," Annie replied, sending her best friend an air kiss across the reception. "You look happy."

Rose's smile grew even wider.

"I am," she said. "Thank you. I'll fill you in on all the goss over cocktails at the weekend."

"Yes, please," Annie said, holding back on her own gossip about Mim. She'd keep that until the weekend too. "Gotta go, don't want the boss to tell me off."

"Yeah you do," Rose replied, winking at Annie. "You crave it."

Rose laughed, gravelly and dirty, and Annie tutted, swiping her pass card to the inner sanctum with her head low so Rose couldn't see her burning cheeks.

Swift had texted first thing to let the team know he'd set up Incident Room One, so Annie bypassed the bullpen open plan office and made her way straight there. Swift was working quietly on his laptop as Annie opened the door and said hi.

"Have you been here all night?" she asked, putting her bag down on the large table and taking out her things.

The room was set up with a white board and notice board at one end, most of the floor space was filled by the oval table and chairs. The blinds were partially drawn to keep out the low sun and rays of light, dotted with a million specks of dust, shone in through the gaps.

Annie stepped around the table to the noticeboard. On the blue felt, Swift had pinned two large photos, one of John Doe, the other of Nicole. Around them was a multi-legged spider diagram of all the names they'd come across so far. She was about to mention her thoughts of the previous guests when Tink and Page burst into the room with laden arms and wide smiles.

"Good morning, team," Page said, dropping his bags on the desk. "I bring gifts."

He turned to Tink who was looking at him with a frown.

"You bring gifts?" Tink carefully placed a couple of paper bags on the desk, and from the waft of cinnamon

and sugar that emanated from the bag, Annie guessed they were full of pastries.

"Yeah," Page grinned. "I bought them. Help yourself, guys."

"I carried them." Tink stood up straight and eyeballed Page.

"But... but you offered to carry them," he said, his face crumpled. "That doesn't mean you get the kudos."

"I always get the kudos," Tink blew Page a kiss and dived into the bag for a cinnamon swirl.

"You're infuriating," Page grumbled, taking one for himself and sitting with a thump on one of the chairs.

Tink pulled out the chair next to him and sat down with a smile and a flake of pastry on the end of her button nose.

"Alright, kids, when you're ready," Swift said, his lips curling upwards at the sight of the breakfast. He peered into the bag and pulled out a maple and pecan slice, putting it carefully on the notepad in front of him. "Okay, so, who's going to talk through what we have?"

Annie looked around at Page and Tink who were already halfway through their breakfast treats, Swift had just taken a large bite of his. They all looked back at her expectantly.

"Oh, alright," she said, getting up from her chair and heading around to the noticeboard.

"You do it so well," Swift said behind his hand, through a mouthful of pastry.

"Charmer." Annie smiled. "Okay, quick recap. Paradise Grove, luxury and exclusive spa retreat. A group of four women celebrating a birthday. We have John Doe our dead man, found with a pair of scissors through his chest on the bed of Nicole, one of the hotel guests, the birthday girl, no less. John Doe was apparently not known to any of the staff or guests, however, we know now that he bribed Dina, the housemaid, to let him in to the grounds on the basis he was surprising Nicole."

Annie walked to the whiteboard and picked up a pen.

"We need to know," she said, pulling the lid off then and writing the questions as she said them. "Who John Doe is? How he knows Nicole. And why he had to sneak into the hotel instead of just booking a day pass."

Annie walked back to the noticeboard.

"All the staff have been accounted for during the attack on John Doe's life. We talked to them yesterday and from the timeline that Page drew up, only Pamela was alone." Annie relayed the conversation she'd overheard from Pamela's office and watched as Tink and Page's faces went from shock to confusion. "But I do think there is something they are all keeping from us. Spencer and Dina are in a relationship and they're vouching for each other, Spencer was very tight-lipped last night, didn't have much to say about anything, and I'm sure Dina fears him. I think she's scared of Misti too, just from an interaction I witnessed yesterday. In fact, I think those three are hiding something from us. I'm not sure what, but they're lying about something."

"Spidey senses?" Swift asked.

"Yep." Annie nodded, going back to the white board. "So we can add to this with questions for the staff. Who was Pamela talking to? What are the staff hiding from us? Page, is there anything you can add after watching Pamela yesterday?"

Page wiped his mouth with the back of his hand and cracked open a bottle of water, swigging quickly. "She's on edge. The whole afternoon yesterday she was back and forth between her office and the games room. But it was weird, I didn't feel like she was going to the games room to check on her staff or the guests. It felt like she was waiting for something, she kept looking out of the window at the front, and down the driveway."

"Interesting," Swift added. "Thanks Page."

Annie underlined Pamela's name and headed back over to the noticeboard.

"And," she said, pointing to the photo of Nicole. "We have a misper. Nicole Cox, abducted in daylight from the middle of a secure hotel. A note was left in her room, with the words *we know what you've done and you're going to pay.* The search has pulled up nothing, and her friends, Olivia Grant-Rose, childhood friend, Joy Burrage and Shelly Took, work friends, are getting frantic. I think this was someone who knew the hotel so I think we should case the previous guests."

"Agreed," Swift added.

"Tink has found some info on Nicole, Tink do you want to take this one?" Annie stood back a bit and gestured to Tink.

Tink nodded, brushing her hands together. "Nicole,

twenty-nine, from Luton. Her parents are well off, they run a business. Something to do with property finance, Nicole used to work for them before she moved in with her boyfriend, and now works part-time in an insurance call-centre. Talking to the list of friends that the boyfriend gave us has imparted no further info on Nicole. It seems as though no-one really knows who she is, deep down. They all referred to her as Ian's wife, which was weird, as I didn't think they were married.

Nicole's parents have been amazing, they're so worried, but have been calling us with any information they have. They say they see less of Nicole now she's moved out of home, that they miss her but that they understand she has to make a life of her own. They've asked for privacy from the press, but we all know how well that normally turns out."

"Hmm," Swift agreed. "Do we know any more about the leaked photo?"

"Not yet," Page answered. "I've called the paper, but they're unable to name their source without a warrant."

"Which we can get but it'll take time and effort and manpower we don't really have in the middle of a murder and a misper case." Swift ran his hands through his hair.

"Ian Coles," Annie went on, wanting to add how she felt about the man they'd gone to meet. "The boyfriend, or husband, we need to find that out really, though I'm not sure what difference it makes. He struck me as an alpha male, I can't imagine he'd be very happy that Nicole had a surprise guest in the form of our John Doe."

"He has a cast iron alibi for the time John Doe was killed." Swift put his hand on a sheet of paper in front of him, Annie didn't need to read it to know it was the written statements of Ian's work alibis. "Also, why would he abduct his own girlfriend?"

Annie wrote Ian Coles on the whiteboard, anyway, putting a question mark after his name. There was something about him she couldn't gel with, and she was sure it was more than past experience of alpha males.

"Okay," Swift said, clapping his hands together. "Page, get the note that we found to forensics, test it for fingerprints, and chase up the tox and lab reports for John Doe and the scissors while you're there. Tink, let's look more into Ian Coles. Find out what you can about his background. I've put a press release out with an image of John Doe's face to see if anyone comes forward. It's been three days now and nothing; either he's a loner which I doubt, given how much emphasis he placed on looks, or he was expected to be away. But the case is pivoting around this man with no identity. Annie, I think we should…"

Swift was interrupted by the chirrup of his phone. He swiped to answer, and the team fell silent, watching as his face paled and slackened.

"Annie, change of plan, we need to go back to the hotel. Something has been washed up on the beach."

THIRTEEN

THEY PULLED ALL THE WAY AROUND TO THE CAR PARK at the side of Paradise Grove and jumped out of the car. The chatter of police radios filled the air and one of the patrol cars had its lights flashing. It lent to an already eerie atmosphere as the low-lying sea mists gathered across the gardens. The lights strobed through the fog like a smoke machine in a club.

"There's a team down on the sand," one of the officers told Swift as he marched over to the car. "They're setting up a cordon, though we're not sure how long we have before the tide comes back in and washes everything away. The Oceanographic Centre data seems to be giving us another three hours, tops."

"Okay, thanks," Swift replied.

"Do you want us to call forensics?" The officer added.

Swift shook his head. "There's no point, the tide would have swept away any evidence, and we can't be sure of where it went into the water or when. We'll bag what we can and send it across to Evans. Remain here and you can blues and twos when we're done."

"Sir." The officer stood down.

"Annie, let's take the quick route," Swift called across to her.

Annie was already way ahead of him; she'd cut over the grass and was halfway to the low fence at the back of the garden. Even before she got to the cliff face, she could hear the roar of the sea, a warning, reminding her that even though the tide was out, it was still there waiting. She shivered and climbed over the fence, dropping to the ledge below. It was wet and her shoes sank into the sand with a squelch. Sliding down the bank, Annie could see a cordon. Blue police tape flapping in the offshore breeze, attached to poles stuck into the sand at jaunty angles. What lay beyond the tape made Annie's heart race up her throat and pulse heavily in her neck.

A bundle of clothes, wet through, dark and heavy with water spread out ominously as though Nicole was still wearing them.

"Are they definitely hers?" Annie asked Swift as he came up alongside her.

"It was Olivia who found them," Swift replied, signalling their arrival to the officer in charge of the scene. "And she was adamant that they belong to Nicole. Said she recognised the pattern on the jumper."

Annie passed under the tape with the nod from Swift. On closer inspection of the dark pile on the sand, she could make out the individual items of clothing.

There was a pair of jeans, Levis, their red tag sticking skywards. A jumper, twisted in assault from the water, the arms wrapped around themselves as though trying to protect. Around the neckline were large oval jewels, not real, Annie guessed, from the Primark label attached to the jumper. Just under the jeans was something else, Annie couldn't quite work out what it was without moving the clothes.

"Is it okay?" she asked Swift, getting down on her haunches to try and get a better view.

"Go right ahead," Swift said. "Olivia moved them all anyway, so she says. She thought it *was* Nicole."

Annie felt a tickle down the back of her neck. From a distance the pile of clothes could have looked like a human being. Poor Olivia, she'd need to go and speak to her to make sure she was okay. But not before checking out what was tucked under the jeans.

Annie brushed her hands down her own trousers and, using just her gloved fingertips, pulled the jeans to the side. Underneath, cracked and dripping with sea water, was the phone that Annie had seen on Nicole's bed stand.

"Swift," Annie said, lifting it up and watching as a torrent of water ran out of the socket at the bottom. "Have you got a bag?"

Swift pulled an evidence bag from his pocket and held it open for Annie to drop the phone in.

"It's not looking good, is it?" he said, peeling the tape from the top of the bag and sealing it shut.

"Is this what Nicole was wearing when she disappeared?" Annie asked. "Only, why remove her jumper and jeans? What about her underwear, or t-shirts, vests, that kind of thing?"

"We'll need to check with Olivia," Swift replied. "She was the last one to see Nicole. Though she knew these were hers, she didn't say if she'd been wearing them on Monday."

Annie stood back up, her knees protesting with the cold and damp that had seeped through her trousers.

"If it's okay," she said, brushing them down. "I'd like to go and speak to Olivia anyway. She must have had a shock, seeing these clothes laid out like this on the beach. I'd like to check she's okay."

"Be my guest," Swift replied. "I'm going to stay here and get these bagged up and make sure they're sent back asap. See you back in the dining room in a bit?"

"Sure." Annie ducked back out under the police tape and started to make her way back towards the sand bank and the fence.

Seeing how wet the sand still was, she changed her mind and her direction, knowing that clambering up the slope with no help would be a fool's game. She headed instead across the sand and around the cove. The police had taken down a section of fencing on either side of the Grove's private land to allow them free access to the beach during their searches. As Annie walked through the gap in the fence she could see, even clearer, how much of a tunnel had been dug through the cliff face where the fence still met the chalky wall. It would have been an escape route for whoever took Nicole, that's for sure, but Annie felt her mind whirring with questions about why across the beach, why not straight out the front?

Annie noticed a couple of people walking towards her as she rounded the cove and headed up the beach towards the road. She wondered if they would be making use of the through-route that had been opened up across the private beach. It was quite a detour if both fences were still intact, all the way up to the driveway of Paradise Grove and across the dunes on the other side, and that's only when the sea was out. At other times the walk would be inaccessible.

Annie followed the line of Paradise Grove's land, marked quite starkly by the high fence. She trod the path as close to the fence as she could, hacking away at some of the overgrowth as she went. Rounding on the carpark, Annie saw just how overgrown it was under-foot. The kind of wild, spiky grass that did well battling the elements this close to the sea, only some of them were already trampled. Flattened right down to the sandy earth, browning at the edges where they had started to die. Annie poked at one of the grasses with her boot, moving it from side to side, watching as the blades fell apart from the stem. This must have been where John Doe stood and waved down Dina.

Annie looked up at the hotel. The view through the fence was clear, all the way down to the driveway and all the way up to the gardens and the very edge of the spa barn. It was a good lookout, one where John Doe would have been able to watch the staff coming and going, waiting for someone he thought he could manipulate well enough to let him in.

A figure cut across the window of the dining room. By the slightness of the frame and the stoop of the shoulders, Annie guessed it was one of the guests. She picked up her pace and marched around the rest of the fence to the entrance of the driveway, and up and in the front door. The coldness that had seeped into Annie's clothes during her time on the beach was replaced with a sweatiness that stuck to her skin; clammy and warm. Annie unzipped her coat and fanned her face.

The games room door to her right was propped open with a stack of books, the three women beyond looked flustered themselves; pink cheeked and shiny. Annie stepped inside the room, thinking she'd see the rest of the staff and a couple of officers too, but it was empty except for the guests. Shelly and Joy huddled together on the sofa, their arms and legs tucked into their bodies, heads down, staring at their phone screens. On an armchair in the corner of the room, Olivia sat alone. Limp, unoccupied, staring into space as though lost in her own thoughts. She was pale, a hollow version of the woman Annie had met before. Her platinum ringlets hung heavily around her unmade face and her eyes looked puffy and red.

"You on your own?" Annie asked, trying not to sound annoyed. There was a killer on the loose and Swift had explicitly asked a uniformed officer to be manning this room at all times.

"Yes," Shelly answered, tucking a lank strand of hair behind her ears. "The officer just got called away."

"Are you all okay?" Annie asked, then she stopped just inside the door, a commotion startling her from the end of the corridor. It was a man's voice, loud and angry, and heading in their direction.

Annie pushed the stack of books away with her foot and let the door close quietly, pushing one of the low coffee tables up against it. She was trying to stay calm, but the noises outside the room grew louder. More voices shouted; low, heated, male voices. Annie could make out one or two different aggressors. She held up a finger to her lips to quieten the women, though there was no need, the shock on their faces was enough to keep them from making a sound. The crackling of a police radio squawked outside the door, followed by a request for assistance as the shouting grew in anger. A glass smashed somewhere along the corridor; a door banged closed. Annie bent down and looked through the keyhole of the games room door.

"What?" she whispered, standing up and pushing the table out of the way.

She indicated to the women to stay where they were and pulled the door open.

"Ray?" Annie said, edging slowly into the corridor, recognising the two men they'd talked to in Market Harpleigh. "Kieran? What's going on here?"

The uniformed officer who had been radioing for back-up, held his hand up to Annie from the other end of the corridor.

"Get back inside the room, Ma'am," he said, sternly. "It's all under control."

"I was just trying to calm him down," the fisherman shouted to Annie over the angry roar coming from the old man. "He's had a bit too much."

Kieran mimicked swigging a pint and Ray spun on his heels to face the fisherman and take a swipe. Luckily for Kieran, the punch missed his face altogether, the momentum spinning Ray all the way around and unbalancing him right into a puzzled Swift's arms.

"Alright, Ray," Swift said, taking it all in his stride. "No need for that now, is there? Let's get you sobered up."

Ray's arms windmilled, whether to have a go at Swift now too, or to stay upright, Annie wasn't sure. Swift held him tighter, dragging him upright by the armpits.

"Unless you'd like a night in the cells, that is?" he added.

"She should be in the bloody cells, not me," Ray slurred. "She won't be happy until *all* of us are dead."

Annie looked in the direction of Ray's anger and saw the scared face of Pamela disappear back into her office.

Until all of us are dead? Was Pamela responsible for John Doe's murder? And why was Ray so sure she would do it again?

FOURTEEN

"IN HERE," SAID SWIFT, HIS VOICE STRUGGLING WITH the weight of the man he was holding up. "Sit down and shut up."

Swift dropped the man on a dining chair and marched across the floor to the coffee machine, stretching out his shoulders as he went. Annie pulled two chairs together on the opposite side of the table to Ray and took one of them. Soon the room was filled with the aroma of fresh coffee which almost drowned out the stench of the cider sweating out of Ray's pores.

A movement caught Annie's eye, it was Dina and Spencer, just beyond the dining room in the kitchen, she could hear them talking in whispered snatches of speech. Drawing herself up from her chair, Annie pushed open the kitchen door to find the two young staff members in what looked like a warm embrace.

"Sorry," she said, as they broke apart from each

other. Spencer's face twisted into a scowl. "But would you mind giving us the space to talk to Ray, here?"

Dina wriggled out of Spencer's arms and straightened her apron.

"Sure," she said, wiping her face. "I need to go and turn down the beds anyway."

Dina scampered past Annie, not meeting her eyes. Spencer squared his shoulders, drawing a smile on his face that was no more real than the coffee Swift was making. The young man motioned to Annie to leave first, but the idea of having her back to him made Annie's skin crawl.

"I don't think so," she said, stepping back and motioning for Spencer to walk first.

The look he gave her in return was colder than the North Sea.

"We won't be too long," Swift said to Spencer, as he crossed the dining room, all smiles now. "Then you and Hans can get back to making the guests supper."

"Nothing to make them," Spencer replied with a tilt of his chin. "The fridges are nearly empty and so are the cupboards. It's been a bit hard to shop while we're all kept prisoner here."

He raised his chin towards Swift who was used to the smart mouths of young men trying to intimidate him. He just smiled back.

"Perhaps you've heard of the internet?" he asked, politely. "Perhaps you could go and do that now, unless you have something better to do?"

Annie watched as Spencer caught Dina's eyes. An

unspoken moment passed between them before Dina hurried off down the corridor. Spencer huffed and followed after her.

Annie sat back down, gratefully taking the coffee Swift had placed on the table in front of her. Ray was sipping his, his face calmed to a cerise pink from the post box red it had been out in the corridor.

"So Ray," Swift started. "This isn't a formal interview or anything like that, but if you prefer, we can talk somewhere else? Your home, perhaps?"

Ray gruffed out an answer which Annie took for an affirmative to stay where he was, given that he didn't move from his chair. Swift must have done the same as he continued talking.

"Just in case you don't remember from the other day, I'm DI Swift and this is Ms O'Malley," Swift said, and Annie slumped a little in her chair.

"Annie," she said pointedly at Ray. "You can call me Annie."

Swift gave her a sideways glance and looked back at Ray.

"Can you tell us what you're doing here at Paradise Grove?"

Ray looked across the table with bloodshot eyes. His hands shook so much, the coffee in his cup trembled as though from an earthquake.

"I came to give that stuck up witch a piece of my mind," he said, gloopily, his lips were so dehydrated they were sticking together.

"And by *stuck up witch*, I'm going to assume you mean Pamela Parris?" Swift asked.

"You've met her too, then?" Ray asked, brightly.

"I assumed you meant Ms Parris by the accusations you were throwing in her direction when we dragged you away." Swift sighed and rolled his eyes.

"Oh," Ray said, dejected again. He licked his lips and took a sip of milky coffee. "Right. Well, yeah, her."

He spat out the word as though she was poison.

"What arguments do you have with Ms Parris?" Annie asked.

Ray lifted an eyebrow at her. "You wouldn't understand."

"Try me," Annie replied, deadpan.

"Market Harpleigh is a ruined town because of this place," Ray said to Swift. "That woman has ruined it by running down the hotel and closing off the beach. A beach which isn't even hers."

Ray was getting riled again, his words increasing in volume, his shoulders pulled back.

"Sit back, Ray," Swift asked, calmly, then waited until Ray had slunk back into his chair. "What were you planning on doing to Pamela when you got here?"

Ray shrugged and gulped down the rest of his coffee, wiping his mouth with the back of a grubby hand. "Dunno. Just heard the gate was open so I thought I'd come up and have a look around, see what *she's* done to run this place into the ground as well as the whole town."

"What do you know about Paradise Grove?" Annie asked him, curious as to why he thinks it's being run into the ground.

"When this place was The Marlborough, it used to bring in all the rich clients who'd hang out in town and spend their money there too," he replied. "And now, according to gospel, it's worthless. No, more than worthless, it's a money pit and that woman is getting funding from the council to save her business when the rest of the town is left to rot. That's not fair. Just look at that man who died? I saw that photo, he was rich, wasn't he? His suit said it all. Why should *she* be given what's rightfully ours?"

Ray pumped his fists against the table making Annie jump. Swift burst from his seat, pushing it out behind him and toppling it with a clatter. He lay his elbows on the table and looked Ray right in the eyes.

"I will ask you once more to calm down, or I will be taking you down to the station and arresting you with… anything." He pushed his arms straight and Annie could see his chest rising and falling.

She bent and picked up Swift's chair, tucking it behind him and he sat down with a thanks.

"Where were you on Monday morning?" Swift asked, quietly.

Ray shuffled on his chair, fiddling with the buttons on his cardigan. "What? Why?"

"Do you have an alibi for the death of the man found here at Paradise Grove?" Swift asked again.

Ray's face drained of cerise and looked like an undercooked pasty. "I was at home. I didn't kill nobody. Why would I kill that man?"

He tugged at the already baggy neck of his t-shirt.

"You just said you thought it was unfair that Ms Parris was being given funding. You then said that man was giving her the funding. That's motive if ever I heard it."

Annie thought Swift was exaggerating slightly, but she'd not linked John Doe to Pamela in those terms before. What if he'd lied about being a surprise for Nicole to get into the hotel? What if he was actually there to meet with Pamela? Why, then, didn't he just call to make an appointment? Or ask Pamela to let him in. If her finances were as dire as Ray was suggesting, maybe Pamela owed the dead man money.

"I was just guessing," Ray said, the reds of his eyes wide with panic. "I don't know if he was, I just thought he looked rich. I would never hurt anyone."

"You threatened Ms Parris just now," Swift said.

"But it's all words." Ray had both his hands on the table, palms down, his bitten nails trembling. "I couldn't never hurt anyone. I was a failed fisherman because I didn't like seeing them flapping about in the nets unable to breathe. Ask anyone."

He flapped his hands a little, above the table, giving the impression of a floundering fish. His mouth opened and closed to enhance his charade.

"We will be, Ray," Swift said. "We will. Now get

out of here before you cause any more damage. Straight home with you."

Ray looked back and forth between Annie and Swift as though it was a test. When he realised he was actually free to go he jumped up quicker than Annie thought possible and headed for the door.

"Actually, one last question, Ray," Annie said as he was about to leave the room. "Who was it who told you the gate to the hotel was unlocked?"

Ray stopped, one leg bent behind him. "Kieran did. He said the whole hotel and beach was open and we should go and check it out."

"Thanks, Ray," Annie said, lifting an eyebrow to Swift as the old man left the room. She picked up her cup and drained the rest of her coffee. "How did Kieran know?"

Swift curled his lips in disregard. "I have no idea. Have you seen him here?"

Annie nodded. "He was trying to calm Ray down before you arrived. Do you really think Ray could be our killer?"

"No," Swift said, tipping his own cup and staring at the dregs in the bottom. "I don't think he's our killer. He doesn't fit the bill. But what he said about Pamela and this place was interesting. Do you think she's in as dire straits as our resident alcoholic makes out?"

"We should look into the finances, definitely," Annie agreed. "And I've thought about our John Doe coming here to see Pamela and not Nicole, but it doesn't make any sense."

"None of this makes any sense." Swift got out of his chair and headed towards the corridor.

"Nope," Annie agreed following him. "But if John Doe did come here to meet Pamela, and it's something to do with money troubles, then why was John Doe found in Nicole's bedroom? Why has Nicole vanished? And why leave a note about Nicole at all?"

"All great questions, O'Malley," Swift said, his shoes clicking on the floor.

"And why do you keep calling me *Ms* O'Malley?" Annie asked, a few steps behind him. "It makes me sound like an old maid."

Swift turned back to Annie with a grin on his face. "Exactly. It's so you can catch people unawares. Ms O'Malley sounds like a crusty school teacher, whereas you're a whizz with people and highly intelligent. I like wrong footing people."

"School teachers are some of the most intelligent people I have ever met," Annie replied, trying to hide her smile. Compliments from Swift were rarer than affordable house prices.

"Wrong analogy then, but you get my meaning?" Swift pulled out his phone and dialled. "Tink, can you look into Paradise Grove's accounts for me, just the last five years if it's available, please? We're on our way back to the city now, and we'll regroup again in the morning. I've expedited all forensics on the case now, so they should be back with us tomorrow. See you then. Oh, and Tink, can you get Page to check to see if we have any previous for a man called Ray who lives in Market Harpleigh. Shouldn't be too hard to find as there are minimal people living there. And let's try Kieran Hucklesby while we're at it."

Swift signed off and ended the call.

"Shall we let Pamela and the guests know we're leaving?" Annie asked as they passed Pamela's closed office door.

"I don't think there'll be any need for that," Swift said, grimly, from the entrance. "We're not going anywhere."

Annie tilted her head at him, stepping up to the open front door and peering outside. The tide had come in. Down the steps and halfway down the driveway she could see Ray crossing the tidal surge as it swept across the tarmac. The sea reached up to his waist and it pulled him about like a rag doll.

"Wait here," Swift said, and he ran down the steps and towards the water. "Ray, don't be an idiot, come back."

Ray waved his arm in dismissal at Swift's shouts.

"I've got to get home to my cat," he yelled back. "She'll go hungry without me."

Annie's heart was in her mouth as the old man fell forwards, his arms splashing maniacally to keep his head above the water. She clenched her fists, daring not to breath. And then he started to rise up the other side of the driveway, clothes soaked through, hair plastered to his head. Swift stopped at the water's edge, and they both watched as Ray toddled down the driveway and back towards Market Harpleigh.

Annie headed back inside, as the shadows fell over the hotel. There was no way the tide would be out in time to drive home for the night. They were stuck here with the guests, the staff, and potentially a killer.

FIFTEEN

FRIDAY

ANNIE AWOKE WITH A START, HER WHOLE BODY TENSE, alert. A sickening feeling grew in her stomach and rose acidly up her throat. Something had woken her. A noise? A crash? A shout? Annie couldn't remember past the fug of sleep. She looked around the room, but everything was black. She held her breath and listened hard, trying to hear past the blood pumping in her ears, but it was no use. Holding her hands up, Annie couldn't even see her fingers wiggling in front of her face.

Breathe.

Taking a few deep breaths, Annie felt her body creak and unwind. Her neck crunched as she moved her body to the side of the bed and reached out an arm, fumbling for the bedside lamp. The light that flooded the hotel room burned Annie's eyes, but she felt a wash of relief as she made out the tightly drawn curtains, the Art Deco wardrobe, and matching dresser, and the little en-suite whose door she had left open in case she'd needed to go in the night.

"What are you doing?" Swift's voice was thick with sleep as he rolled over and grunted, pulling his duvet over his head. "It's the middle of the night."

Somehow, despite the hotel being practically empty, Swift and Annie had ended up sharing a twin room. Pamela had said it would be easier on Dina and Gloria given how tired they both were, and she didn't want them to be traipsing up and down the stairs twice if once would do it. Not that it bothered either Annie or Swift, not until now, anyway.

"It's half five," Annie replied, looking at her watch. She threw her covers back and swung her legs out of bed, rubbing her face awake and heading across the room to the bathroom. "And I heard something."

"What did you hear?" came Swift's muffled voice from under the covers.

"I don't know, do I?" Annie shouted through the closed bathroom door. "I'm going to investigate. Right after I've peed. Priorities."

She flushed the toilet and washed her hands and face, wracking her brains to try and filter what had been a dream and what had been reality. There *had* been a noise, she was sure of it. Leaving the bathroom and heading back into the bedroom, Swift was already out of bed and back in his clothes.

"What are *you* doing?" Annie asked, tiptoeing back to her bed and grabbing yesterday's clothes from the floor where she'd dropped them.

"You don't think I'm letting you go wandering off around Paradise Grove after hearing a strange noise, do you?" Swift asked. "Not after everything that's happened."

"I didn't realise I needed your permission to go for a walk," Annie said, spikily.

"Oh no, you don't" Swift replied. "But you're not leaving me here on my own in the dark to fend for myself."

Annie laughed. Swift moved to the window and peeked out the curtains. "Why *is* it so dark out here?"

"No streetlights." Annie ran her fingers through her hair and tied it back off her face. "Now come on, before whatever made the noise disappears and the sun comes up."

They were up on the top floor of the hotel. Creeping down the back staircase, Annie pushed open the door to the first-floor corridor. It was empty. Police tape sealed off Nicole's room and the other three doors were shut tight. Annie wondered if the women beyond them were asleep, or if they lay awake worried about their friend. It seemed strange to her, a small group of four celebrating a milestone birthday, with two of those friends being people Nicole worked with. Annie had gotten the impression that Nicole was well liked, kind, and caring. So where were all her close, long-term friends? School friends? University friends? Even if Nicole had only wanted to celebrate with a select few, from the list Tink was going through, Nicole didn't have a very big selection to choose from.

She shut the door again, slowly and quietly, and shook her head at Swift, motioning for him to head down to the ground floor. Tiptoeing slowly, Annie followed Swift down the stairs, stopping when they got to the corridor that split, one way to the glass walkways to the spa, the other around to the front of the hotel.

"That way," Annie said, pointing to the hotel, aware that they'd spent little to no time in the spa since arriving. So much for working it out in the steam room. "I don't think someone making a noise in the spa would have woken me up."

The sound of a door opening and closing stopped them in their tracks. Swift held up his finger to his lips, hushing Annie. She could hear a rustle of paper at the far end of the corridor, footsteps. Now was there chance. Swift hurried quietly up the corridor, Annie hot on his heels. She saw him reach for his side pocket, hand hovering in case he needed quick access to his phone. Stopping at the foot of the stairs, they listened out for any more signs of movement. They had an advantage over whoever was stalking the corridors this early in the morning, neither of them was wearing shoes, and their socks made no noise on the floorboards. The footsteps started up again, receding away from where the detectives had stopped.

Swift turned back to Annie, raising his brows in question. Annie knew him well enough to know he was asking if she was ready? She gave him a thumbs up and drew breath, her limbs poised and ready for action. Swift peered around the stairs, lifting an arm and then dropping it.

They ran forwards; the corridor was steeped in darkness, heavy lidded, not yet woken, but Annie caught a glimpse of the back of a head walking away, heading for the dining room. They ran silently towards the figure, coming up behind just as they reached out their hand to open the door.

"Not so fast," Swift said, grabbing the wrist of the figure.

Annie's stomach tumbled over itself with a wash of nausea. Was this the killer, still wandering the corridors? Should they have held back to see if they could have been led to Nicole? Her jumbled questions were put to an abrupt end with the angry shouts of their apprehended intruder.

"Get off me, what do you think you're doing?"

Swift stood back, treading on Annie's toes.

"Sorry," he whispered to Annie, as the hallway lights flickered on above their heads.

"What is the meaning of this?" Pamela Parris stood, hands on the hips of her dressing gown, glaring at Swift.

There was a stack of letters in one of her hands, and the morning paper in the other.

"Sorry," Annie said, noticing the eye mask pushed back on Pamela's head. "We... well, I heard a noise. We were just checking it out. I wasn't expecting others to be up so early."

"A hotel never sleeps," Pamela shot back. "The noise you heard was the letter box. I have to get up early to pick it up so none of our guests see the... the mail."

Pamela spun on her heels and pushed through to the dining room. She headed straight for the coffee machine and flicked on the switch at the wall. Dropping the mail and the newspaper, Pamela grabbed the water container and marched through to the kitchen. Annie pulled a face at Swift as the tap splashed noisily from the other room.

"There's a post box at the gate," Annie whispered. "The noise wasn't the post box waking me, it must have been Pamela opening and closing the front door."

"Check the mail," Swift mouthed, edging to the kitchen door and looking inside. "Quick."

Annie picked up the pile of letters from the table and started flicking through them. The top few were bills, and not the general monthly statements, these were all red topped and demanding payment. There weren't just a handful either, this was a thick stack of calls for payment. Slipped in between the last angry bill and the newspaper was a thick cream envelope, Annie glanced up at Swift who was still watching the kitchen, then pulled it out from the pile. The envelope wasn't stamped, only Pamela's name printed on the front in scratchy pen, no address, nothing. Annie turned it over in her hand. It wasn't sealed either. She pulled out the slip of paper, recognising the thick, black pen scrawled across the page.

We know what you've done. Pay up, or
you'll be sorry.

"What are you doing with that?" Pamela strode out of the kitchen, a grey catering tray full of small white mugs clattered in her hands. She put it down on the table next to Annie with such force, there were sure to be more than a couple of casualties. With perfectly manicured fingers, Pamela ripped the note and envelope from Annie's grasp and screwed them into a tiny ball. "You should know it's *illegal* to open other people's mail."

"That's not mail, Pamela," Annie said. "That's blackmail."

Swift crossed the room in three giant strides.

"Annie?" he asked.

"Hand delivered." Annie took Pamela's hands in hers and carefully peeled open her fingers, taking out the mess of note and envelope and handing it to Swift. "Written in the same hand as the note we assumed was about Nicole's disappearance."

Swift untwisted the note, discarding the envelope on the table, and read it out loud. Pamela exhaled, her whole body diminishing in front of Annie. She staggered forward, a hand reaching out to steady herself on the table. Annie pulled out a chair and helped Pamela to sit down before she injured herself.

"Do you want to tell us what's going on?" Annie asked, perching on the table in front of Pamela.

Pamela sighed and dropped her head into her hands, grabbing fistfuls of hair so it looped tightly around her knuckles. Up close, Annie could see the abundance of grey roots poking out of Pamela's scalp, a defined line between natural and the block of dyed hair. For reason's she couldn't figure out, it made Annie feel a tug of sadness for the woman sitting in front of her. As though her battles were all defeating her, slowly dragging her down.

"I may as well tell you," Pamela said, her voice muffled under her hands. "Everyone hates me already, what's a few extra angry voices added to the mix?"

Letting go of her hair, Pamela rubbed at her face, pulling her dressing gown tighter around her body.

"Go on," Swift said, softly. "We're not here to judge. We just want to find out where Nicole is and what happened to the dead man in her room."

"You have to trust me when I say I have no idea on either of those points." Pamela's gaze was steely, though she looked at neither Annie nor Swift.

Annie followed her line of sight out the window and across the carpark to the fence.

"But that note," Annie said, trying to bring Pamela's attention back into the room. "The note we thought was about Nicole, it wasn't was it?"

The older woman shook her head slowly, her eyes brimming with tears.

"I'm really sorry," she said, as a single drop tracked

down her cheek. She wiped it away hastily, catching the corner of her eye with her watch and wincing. "I had to think fast because I couldn't let my staff know the note was directed at me. Spencer saw me with it and I just panicked and said I found it in Nicole's room."

Annie could see Swift in the corner of her eye, she could tell he was getting annoyed, quite rightly given the note had changed the course of their search from a missing person to an abduction. She hoped he'd stay quiet long enough to let Pamela finish her story.

"Who is sending you these notes?" Annie asked.

"I don't know," Pamela confessed, stroking the crumpled note with a finger, tracing the writing as though the ink may give up its secrets. "I think it must be some of the people who live in Market Harpleigh. You've seen how much they love me!"

"You think they're sending you notes because of the access to the beach?" Annie asked, remembering how angry both Roy and Kieran had seemed about the fence.

Pamela laughed, a bark of a laugh that startled Annie. Her eyes had darkened, though the sun was starting to rise in the sky and filter through the windows in the dining room.

"The beach is fenced off for *their* safety." Pamela ran a hand through her hair, twisting the strands that fell by her cheek. "You've seen how close the spa is to the edge of the cliff. It's only a matter of weeks before that is having to close, though no one knows it yet."

Annie felt a chill wrap around her neck like a scarf. She knew she'd been right to feel anxious about the barn as it balanced precariously on the cliff edge, enticed ever closer to the sea by the rising tide.

Swift's phone broke the silence that ensued, he excused himself and took off out into the carpark

"Ever since I took over this place," Pamela went on. "It's been a crumbling mess just waiting to meet its watery grave. Dad left the beach open because he knew it would draw in the locals as well as his paying guests, more money for the bar if they all had easy access to the Grove, or the Marlborough as it was then. But I couldn't take that risk with people's lives. The cliff used to break away in huge chunks. I only put the fence up to protect them, yet they hate me for being exclusive. I can't win. I've known that for a while now. Which is why I've got Paradise Grove up for sale. Next month I'm moving to a flat in North London and I can't wait."

Annie's eyebrows hit her hairline. That wasn't what she'd been expecting. She was about to say as much when Swift burst back into the room, his phone still clasped in his hand.

"That was Page," he said, loudly. "I think we need to get your staff down here for a little chat, Pamela."

"What's happened?" asked Annie, hopping down from the table.

"The lab results are back on the scissors," Swift replied, heading out into the corridor. "And there's a match for the cleaning fluid from the hotel kitchen."

"Of course," Pamela replied, confused, chasing after the DI. "Whoever killed him probably took it on their way through the hotel, that doesn't mean it was my staff."

"But that's not all," Swift went on, not turning back. "Fingerprints are back on the note we sent to the lab. And they're positive for Spencer."

"Well of course they are," Pamela replied, hurriedly, catching up to Swift and trying to get past him. "I handed him the note when I was pretending I had just found it."

Swift stopped abruptly and turned back to Pamela.

"Can you explain to me, then, why his fingerprints were found *underneath* the ink?"

SIXTEEN

THE SUN WAS HIGH IN THE SKY BY THE TIME ALL THE staff were rounded up. The dining room was a hubbub of activity, laden with the heavy presence of the search party. Four officers grouped together around a man with a neat beard and a clipboard.

Annie didn't feel particularly reassured at the sight of them, not with the revelation that the note wasn't about Nicole. It was four days since John Doe was found in Nicole's room and Annie felt no further on in their quest to find out who he was and why he was killed, let alone who killed him. All avenues were now pointing firmly in the direction of Paradise Grove itself, but Annie couldn't shake the feeling that they were missing something important.

"So the original note had nothing to do with Nicole, then?" Tink asked Annie, as they stood watching the staff enter the dining room. "Page updated me on the forensics. Did you and Swift sleep well?"

Annie looked across at Tink, who had a wry smile on her face.

"Like babies," Annie replied, not rising to the bait. "And yes, it changes things rather. I'm not sure what the operational decisions of the task force will look like now. Do you?"

Tink motioned for Annie to step back into the kitchen, away from the team members gathering around Swift and Pamela.

"Nicole is now a person of interest," Tink said, in a low voice. "DCI Robins has sent the CPS evidence so we can get a warrant to search her property."

"God, really?" Annie gasped. "Does Swift know?"

Tink grimaced. "I told him when I got here. He wasn't a happy bunny."

"I'm not surprised."

Tink shrugged, tucking a strand of hair behind her ear. "Robins just wanted to make sure we're not having to wait for the CPS when the time comes to arrest Nicole. It's all red tape and bureaucracy, you know that Annie."

Annie sighed; she had thought Robins was different. But in this job—in any job—management always had their own backs. It was bureaucratic, but that was no reason to go over Swift's head and order a warrant; Robins could have spoken to the team first.

They made their way through into the dining room where the atmosphere had dropped to fridge-like temperatures. No one was sitting down. Swift and Pamela stood side by side in front of the door to the carpark. Spencer looked like he was squaring up to them, his stance threatening; legs wide, arms crossed. Dina, Gloria, and Hans made up the rest of the semi-circle that enclosed the DI and the Paradise Grove manager.

"If it's not enough to keep us here like prisoners, you have to keep asking questions over and over and over." Spencer's body tilted towards Swift when he spoke. "If you were all doing your jobs properly, you wouldn't need to keep asking us the same questions. It's not our fault you're all incompetent."

Annie could see the pulse in Swift's temple, a tell-tale sign of his mounting annoyance. But she knew him well enough to know he could control his temper better than anyone else she'd met. Which was more than could be said for Spencer, whose voice was rising as quickly as the red rash creeping up his neck.

"We have some new evidence." Annie stepped in, heads turning in her direction. "Which has given us cause to believe that some of you aren't being honest with us. We're not incompetent, we are methodical, there's a huge difference. I'd say incompetence was more akin to leaving fingerprints on a piece of evidence, wouldn't you, Spencer?"

Spencer's mouth opened and closed like cod fish. His face screwing up with the effort of trying to find some words.

Swift helped him out.

"Do any of you recognise this?" He held up the note that Pamela had received that morning. It was bagged as evidence, but still visible through the cellophane.

"What the hell's that?" Spencer asked. "Why would we recognise it?"

Watching from the outskirts, Annie noticed Dina's head drop.

"It's like the note you found in Nicole's room, Pam," Gloria said, pushing her glasses up her nose to see it better. "What do they mean 'we know what you've done'? Who's got to pay up?"

Hans shrugged at Gloria's question and Misti's concentration was far from the room, her gaze dragged out the windows and over to the spa barn.

"Exactly," Swift replied. "It's like the note we thought was found in Nicole's room. But we now have reason to believe that, that note, and this one, are actually destined for Pamela and nothing to do with Nicole. Spencer, you knew about the note, Pamela gave it to you when she found it, there would be no reason for you to deny that."

"And?" Spencer looked like a mouse caught in a cat's pounce.

Swift straightened up, pulling his shoulders back, and rolling his head on his neck.

"There is a woman missing." The clarity of his voice carried over the dining room so clearly that it pulled all the rest of the noises into a vacuum. "We would like any of you who know anything about these *notes* to come forward so we can sort out what is important here. Do you understand?"

Gloria and Hans nodded, they looked as baffled as Annie had upon the realisation of the real intended recipient of the note. Dina stepped out from behind Spencer and started to speak.

"I think I might..." she began.

Spencer whipped an arm across her chest, trying to push her back behind the bulk of his body.

"You don't need to do this, Dee," he said, saccharine sweet.

"Are you going to then?" Dina asked, throwing his arm away and crossing her own. "Because I think we need to."

"There's nothing to tell," Spencer spat, turning to Swift. "She doesn't know what she's talking about."

Dina's face twisted into incomprehension. "Oh for God's sake, Spence, I saw you writing them. You think you're quiet and discrete, but the way you breath loudly with intent whenever you do something that annoys you even remotely, gives you away."

Spencer's face swelled like a prune soaked in brandy. He spluttered a few sounds that might have been the forming of words, but they made no sense to Annie. Or Swift, from the look on his face. The rest of the team stood in stunned silence.

"Spencer," he said. "Do we need to take you in to the station? Or are you happy to tell us the truth here and now so we can give our full attention to Nicole's disappearance?"

"You're all looking at me as though I'm the bad guy, here," he choked. "But it's all her fault."

He pushed his arm out and pointed a finger at Pamela.

"Spencer?" Annie cautioned him. "Time for Nicole is already at a premium. Cut to the point."

Spencer spun on his heels and narrowed his eyes at Annie.

"Pamela Parris is a sell out," he said. "She's getting rid of this place at the first opportunity and running off to the city."

"Which is her prerogative," Annie said, exasperated. "Pamela doesn't owe you a job, Spencer."

"But where else am I supposed to go for work? I've given my all to this place, and she's handing it over to some investor who's going to rip it down and build holiday huts and a bunch of amusement arcades."

This was news to Annie, but really, what Pamela wanted to do with Paradise Grove was her own business.

"That will bring an income to the town, surely?" she asked.

"Not the kind of income we need," Spencer screwed up his nose. "I'd rather the town stayed quiet than become overrun by *those* kind of holiday makers."

The sound of a door banging out in the carpark made their heads all turn in that direction. There was no-one there, the car park was empty of people, the bushes beyond the fence were blowing wildly in the wind that was picking up. Annie's phone buzzed in her pocket, but she ignored it as Spencer restarted his diatribe.

"It wasn't all my idea," he spat, his narrow eyes turning towards Misti. "I only know all this because of *her*."

Misti rolled her eyes and picked at a long, painted nail with her teeth.

"My older brother heard it on the town grapevine," she said. "He's a fisherman, but he's going for a job in the arcade."

"And your brother is?" Swift asked.

"Kieran," Misti replied. "He was here last night with that old guy who lives next to the shops. Ray."

Annie felt the cogs click into place. That's why she felt Kieran had been so familiar, and now she knew why, it seemed obvious. They had the same uninterested face, the same tanned skin and hazelnut eyes. Even the way Misti was holding herself, as though she had a million and one better places to be, was exactly how Kieran had stood back in the harbour.

Swift nodded, returning his attention to Spencer. "So Kieran tells Misti, who tells you, that Paradise Grove is up for sale and your initial reaction is to black-mail Pamela? What are you? Twelve?"

Spencer snorted. "Whatever."

There was something not quite right about this whole saga. There was still a dead man and a missing woman, and Annie was starting to wonder if neither of them had anything to do with the hotel or its staff.

Gloria pulled out a chair from the nearest table and sat down with a slump, offering the chair beside her to

Hans. She looked like she'd seen this drama all before and was well and truly sick of it.

"What were you hoping to gain? And what happened to make it all go so wrong?" Swift asked Spencer.

"What do you mean?" he replied, his face still screwed up. "I was hoping to gain cash from Pamela, so Dina and I could finally move into the city and start over, seeing as neither of us will have jobs soon. It wouldn't have gone wrong if that dead man hadn't shown... Wait a minute, you don't think I have anything to do with that do you?"

Swift's forehead wrinkled and he let out a long huff of a breath.

"You're blackmailing Pamela," he said. "That's not such a great leap, is it? If the man had something to do with the sale of the hotel you might have wanted to stop it for good. The scissors were from the hotel kitchen, which you have access to."

Spencer's nostrils flared, he started to back away from Swift with short, sharp movements.

"Don't, Spencer," Annie said, softly behind him, and he flew around so quickly Annie could feel the cold air propelled towards her.

Shaking his head, his hands at his mouth, Spencer stepped again towards Annie. He wasn't looking where he was going, the only focus he seemed to have was the need to escape from the dining room. In a staccato of movements, Spencer lashed out, pushing away anyone who got in his path out of the room. Annie stumbled backwards into Tink, and the pair landed with a thump on an empty table. Page reached out a muscly arm to try and stop the young barman but was met with an open hand to the face, Spencer's spindly fingers swiped at Page's eyes.

"Spencer," Annie shouted, hauling herself up from where she'd squashed Tink. "It's okay, we just want to talk to you."

"No, no, no, no." Spencer kept repeating the words over and over and over, as he ran down the corridor towards the front door to the hotel.

"Now look what you've done," Dina shouted. "There's no way Spencer would have killed someone. He's a knob sometimes, but he's not a killer. That dead man, he's got nothing to do with Paradise Grove, I told you that. He was here to see Nicole. He told me he was a surprise for the birthday girl. Now leave us alone."

Dina stormed out of the dining room, slamming a chair out of her way, and picking up the pace as she hit the corridor. Moments later the front door slammed, shaking the pictures on the walls.

"That went well!" Hans chuckled, as he slunk off to the kitchen with a shake of his wiry hair. It was the first time Annie had heard him speak, and he spoke the truth.

She scanned the room for Tink, wanting to apologise for squashing her, but something else caught her eye. Across the carpark, through the windows, Annie saw the outline of a woman walking in the direction of the cliff edge. With her coat done up and her hood pulled over her head, she wasn't sure which of the guests it was, only that she walked with purpose towards the sea.

Annie forgot all about her quest to find Tink, instead she wrapped her cardigan around her body and headed out the door to follow.

SEVENTEEN

THE WIND WAS PICKING UP, BRINGING WITH IT THE CHILL of Autumn. Normally this heralded the feeling of new beginnings, the possibilities, the start of new terms and the shirking of old summer skin. But in the tourism industry, September brought uncertainty. And with Paradise Grove up for sale, the uncertainty was spreading its fingers across the whole of Market Harpleigh.

Annie walked across the carpark to the gardens. She felt the tip of her nose start to grow cold and drew her arms around her chest, hugging her hands under her cardigan. The figure was at the cliff edge now, climbing the fence, and dropping down to the ledge below. There was no hesitation, Annie guessed that whoever it was escaping the hotel to the beach had taken this route before.

They weren't doing anything wrong, but Annie

followed anyway, keen to see who it was and find out what they were doing. With one of their party already missing, and time ticking down rapidly, Annie knew the chances of finding Nicole alive were slim, especially now they knew that the demand for money wasn't on offer for the safe return of the birthday girl. The spirits of Nicole's friends would be low, and Annie didn't want them doing anything to hurt themselves while they waited for news of their friend. Trauma had a way of numbing even the surest of minds. It made unhealthy decisions in the wisest of people, increased risky behaviours in the sensible, and these women were not only missing their friend, they had the memories of a dead body to contend with too.

Remembering her phone buzzing earlier, Annie drew it from her pocket and skim read the top of the message from her home page. It was another reply from Mim. Annie's heart thudded loudly in her chest, as though it was trying to escape. There had been a few back and forth messages between the two of them and Annie had savoured every one. She didn't want to read the rest, not right now when her mind was so overwhelmed with the case. If she made it home later, she'd read it then with a glass of red and a pizza from Pete. Her stomach growled at the thought of pizza, but she kept on towards the cliff edge, shivering as the wind found all the gaps in her knitted cardigan.

"Here." Annie felt something soft and warm wrap around her neck and block out the coolness. Swift patted her shoulder and walked alongside her. "You looked cold."

"Thanks," Annie replied, taking the ends and wrapping them around her neck so the scarf was covering all the way up to her chin. "I felt cold too."

The grey cashmere smelt like Swift. It not only warmed her up, but made her feel comforted, homely, and something else that Annie didn't want to dwell on.

"What're you up to?" Swift asked, as they walked.

"I saw someone out here," Annie told him. "They were heading this way. Over the fence where we've been accessing the beach. I couldn't see who it was, I just wanted to make sure they were okay. Something about them looked... I don't know, low, anxious."

"That's kind of you," Swift said. "Did Spencer hurt you just then?"

"Not at all," Annie replied, reaching the fence. She put her hands on the top and stepped up the first rung, swinging her leg over it and dropping down. "But I think I might have hurt Tink. I landed right on top of her! Has Spencer been caught?"

Swift climbed over right behind her, saying something that was whipped away by the wind. Annie could have sworn it sounded like *lucky Tink* but that would make no sense, would it? She didn't say anything as she waited on the sand for Swift to slide down next to her.

"The officer at the door stopped him," Swift said as he regained his balance after a faster than normal slide. "He's in with Page now, I tried to talk to him, but he's so panicked he was making no sense."

Annie brushed down her hands and started to walk towards the lone figure. With the sea out as far as it would go, they looked minuscule against the horizon. They were heading right, in the direction of Market Harpleigh, away from the path back around to the car park, away from the manmade gap in the cliff face. Annie and Swift walked towards the figure, occasionally bumping arms as they stumbled on the sand.

"Do you think he's responsible?" Annie asked, hearing a voice carried towards them on the wind. "Spencer, I mean."

"For the murder?" Swift asked, Annie nodded. "My gut is telling me no. But those letters he sent to Pamela were riddled with hatred, it's hard to tell what someone's like underneath their layers, isn't it? Once he's calmed down, I'm going to send him to the station to formally interview him. I'd like you to be there too."

"Sure," Annie agreed. "Were there more letters than the two we've seen?"

"Piles of them in Pamela's office. Apparently, they'd been increasing in number and aggression over the last two weeks."

"All because he wants to get away from here and buy a house with Dina," Annie said, with an ironic laugh. "You think the fact the Grove is being sold would be a good reason for them both to leave and not get angry about it? That's their aim anyway."

"Hmm," Swift agreed. "You'd think. Can you stop a second?"

Annie stood still, glancing over at Swift who was

staring right at her. Her whole body contracted with anticipation. Swift leaned in towards her, his mouth slightly open. Annie's breath stopped short of her throat, squeezed in her lungs by the tightened muscles.

"Listen?" Swift said, holding his finger up to his lips. "What's that?"

Annie couldn't hear anything over the loud rushing of blood in her ears and the embarrassed internal voice telling her she was an idiot for thinking Swift was about to declare feelings for her. Of course, he wasn't, only a few days ago he'd basically told her he'd been driving his wife around in his car with their dogs.

"Urgh." The sound was out of her mouth before she could stop it.

"Everything okay, O'Malley?" Swift asked, looking at her curiously. "You've gone a weird colour. Is the scarf a bit too tight?" He made motions around his own face, only heightening her embarrassment.

"Yeah," she laughed, and pulled the scarf a little looser. "Sorry, what was it you thought you heard?"

As she stopped talking, Annie heard it herself. The high-pitched, hurried shouts from the figure as she called for her friend. Like the sad cry from a seagull, the voice carried across the wet sand, crisp and haunting. Annie felt her arms prickle with goose bumps, and felt a pang of guilt at being so distracted by Swift and Mim when these women were missing their best friend.

"Come on," Annie called to Swift. "She sounds like she needs our help."

She picked up speed, running across the sand, glad

that the further out she went the harder the sand became. The figure was almost at the edge of the water, close to where the fence disappeared under the waves. Annie hadn't been in this direction, but it was in less of a state of good repair than the other. The fence had large gaps in the chain links, and it sagged at the top from what looked like years of being climbed. Beyond the fence, back towards the land, Annie could see the swell of the cliffs, the coves, and a large opening into the cliff face, the cave that loomed over the groynes like a tidal wave.

"Hey," Annie called to the figure. "Are you okay?"

Her words were scooped up by the offshore winds and dragged back towards the cliff.

"Stop," Swift shouted louder. "Please, stop."

The figure didn't turn back, she kept on walking towards the water, shouting for her friend. A wave broke on the shore, splashing up her legs but still she kept on walking. Annie started to sprint, pumping her arms and legs as hard as she could to propel herself against the sand. Another wave broke, this one now reached up to the figure's waist.

"Stop," Annie shouted again. "Hey."

It worked, she turned around and Annie saw the pale, pinched face of Olivia, Nicole's best friend. She didn't acknowledge the two detectives running towards her, turning back to the sea and shouting. Annie could see the rolling waters, a wash of white-tipped waves crashing towards the shore, impelled along by the winds that were pushing her back. There was no time, the waves would topple Olivia, that much was certain. And whether Olivia had the strength to swim against them, Annie didn't want to wait to find out. With one last push, her lungs and legs burning with the effort of running through sand thick with water, Annie reached out an arm and grasped what she could between her fingers. Pulling hard, Annie yanked Olivia backwards by her jumper and they both fell to the ground, the cold water shocking Annie's body into spasm as the tail end of the large waves lapped gently at the shore.

"Annie," Swift was beside her, kneeling in the water. "Are you okay?"

"I'm fine, I'm fine," Annie gasped, her teeth clattering together. "Check Olivia."

Swift vanished from Annie's view and she dropped her head back down and stared up at the sky. A lone sea bird drifted high above her, circling effortlessly on the wind. Her whole body ached with the cold; her brain felt as though it was freezing inside her skull it stung so much. Colours seemed vivid, crisper than normal. Annie dragged herself to her feet, worry setting in that she was about to have a stroke. She saw Swift kneeling next to Olivia, shivering. He'd wrapped his jacket around the woman and was coaxing her to stand up. Waves were lapping at her feet, but she was stuck fast, staring out into the wide North Sea, still shouting for her friend. The sight made Annie's throat constrict with horror.

"Olivia," she said, her own teeth chattering loudly. "Can you stand up? Can we take you and get you warm? Nicole will need you to be okay, she wouldn't want you to hurt yourself to find her, you're her best friend."

Olivia's face had turned translucent, each of the veins stood out like they'd been drawn with a child's pen. Annie took Olivia's arm as best she could with her own hands starting to numb with the cold, and together she and Swift lifted Olivia to her feet. The words quietened, Nicole's name just a murmur on Olivia's blue lips. But before she stopped talking altogether Olivia took a stuttered breath.

"It's Ian," she muttered in barely a whisper. "It's all Ian. He made Nic get married in secret, and now he's forcing her to try for a baby. He's done all this, he has to be the one to blame."

As they hauled her back across the sand, towards the path that would lead them back around to the carpark, Annie felt Olivia's body become heavier in her arms, as though the weight of what she had just said was pulling her down. Annie felt the tangled threads of the case start to unravel themselves, something about what Olivia had just said had triggered a response in Annie, and she knew that there was a clue in those words.

"We have to bring the boyfriend in," Annie said, across the top of Olivia's head.

"He's got an alibi," Swift whispered back.

"He knows something," Annie said, pointedly.

"Okay, okay, I'll call Tink" Swift agreed, slipping his phone out of his pocket with his free hand and staring at the screen. "Well I never, Evans has messaged. We've got an ID for our John Doe."

EIGHTEEN

"Your man is called Justin Sloan," Evans said over the car speakers, as Swift reversed out of his space and drove out of the gates of Paradise Grove.

Olivia was warming up in a hot bath, her care passed over to the safe hands of Tink, with strict instructions to call a doctor if she fell ill, and to quiz her about her dislike of Ian if she didn't. Page was in charge of Spencer; Annie could see the DC out the windshield loading the barman into the back of a cruiser to travel to the station. Pamela had been left to pick up the pieces of her team which, given the circumstances, was probably the worst job out of the lot of them. But she had to face up to a future without Paradise Grove, they all did.

The speed at which it was being reclaimed to the sea had been shocking to Annie, but these people all lived this life, they knew the power of the water and couldn't have worked at the hotel without knowing their time was coming to an end. While Annie and Swift had been on the beach, Hans had busied himself in the kitchen, making Joy and Shelley and the rest of his team scrambled eggs and toast for brunch, heralding a kind of renewed camaraderie amongst the people left there.

Bumping the car down the driveway and away from the North Sea, Annie listened to the car phone as Evans talked about their John Doe.

"He was twenty-seven," the pathologist continued, his voice tinny over the speakers. "A local lad."

"How did you find him?" Annie asked, holding on to the handle on the roof as Swift sped around a tight corner and towards the main road back into the city.

"A bit of sleuthing," Evans laughed. "Don't worry, I'm not after your job. Wouldn't catch me working with the living, not over my dead body. They're all far too entitled for me, I prefer a body who talks to me with evidence and not greed."

"Right," Annie replied, raising an eyebrow at Swift who grinned. "And Justin Sloan spoke with evidence then, did he?"

"That he did." Annie heard a rustle of papers and the tapping of computer keys. "Here we go. Do you remember the surgical scars I showed you during the autopsy?"

"Yep," Annie and Swift answered in unison.

"I input the surgery they could have come from and a rough age into the system. It took a while, but we whittled it down to a couple thousand men."

"A couple *thousand?*" Annie was shocked.

"Yeah." Evans laughed. "I told you it was a common type of surgery. We looked at location next, which took it to the hundreds. Then with rough height and weight which they always measure pre-op, and Bob's your uncle."

"Has he always been local?" Swift asked.

"Looks that way."

"Anything else you can tell us about him?" Annie asked, keen to learn more about their mystery dead man.

"He's in good shape, other than the stab wound. Looks after himself, which we could tell from his body. But lab and tox results are back in and his organs were in tip top condition too, no alcohol use or drug use prior to death, and no traces found either, which makes me think he wasn't a user. Of drugs anyway, alcohol wears off quicker than most drugs. Barely had an NHS record, the only regular item on his patient summary were bi-monthly STI checks. So, I'd say he was probably single."

"Sounds like it," Swift said, smiling at Annie. "Thanks Evans. Can you drop me a pin to his address, we're on our way now?"

"Will do. Swift, Annie, pleasure as always, and good luck." Evans ended the call and the car fell into a comfortable silence, the road passing under the tyres with a rhythmic thudding.

Moments later Swift's Satnav beeped, and a red pin appeared on the map, indicating a spot on the other side of the city. Swift hit the cruise control and relaxed back into his seat.

"Annie," he said. "Talk me through what we've got, on our way, I need to straighten things out in my head."

"Me too," Annie said. "I was so sure that it was all to do with the Grove, what with the atmosphere with the staff and the way they looked as though they were hiding something from us."

"Which they were."

"Yeah," Annie agreed. "Not murder though, just a bit of blackmail. Poor Pamela."

"She should have told her staff about the sale, really. Given how close they all are and how soon it's all happening."

"Yeah, I hope you'd give me plenty of notice if you were planning on disbanding the MCU."

Swift sucked at his teeth. "Well, actually, Annie…"

Annie laughed and tapped Swift on the shoulder lightly with the back of her hand.

"But in all seriousness," Annie went on. "What Spencer did to Pamela is wrong; will it go to court?"

"Yeah." Swift was concentrating on the road as they came off the dual carriageway and headed towards Evans' pin. "Bandied next to murder it seems harmless enough, but it's a criminal offence. And a pretty horrible one, at that."

The roads grew narrower, windier; Annie grabbed hold of the handle above the door again as she bounced in her seat.

"So if the notes and the staff behaviour have nothing

to do with our dead man Justin Sloan, then the murder and the blackmail are two very separate issues." Annie chewed at the inside of her cheek. "It just seems a bit of a coincidence. And if you've taught me anything this past year, it's that coincidences are rarer than they seem."

"I feel like I need to watch what I say more," Swift said, grinning at Annie. "If you're going to repeat my wise words back to me, they need to actually be wise."

Annie laughed again. "So did you not mean what you said about coincidences?"

"No, I did. And you're right, there is something to all this, something that connects the dots."

"I think our answers might lie with Justin Sloan," said Annie, thinking back to the prostrate form of the man, spreadeagled on the bed in Nicole's room. "Where does he fit in all of this?"

"You think he'll answer all our questions?" Swift asked, as the high hedges dropped away and gave view to the low shorn wheat fields, dotted with teetering stacks of hay bales.

"Hmm." Annie nodded unconvincingly, staring out her window at the fields as they whizzed past.

The trees were turning yellow, their edges crisping and curling, and soon they'd shed their leaves and be just the brittle bones for the winter months. It made no sense to Annie, how they removed their covering for the coldest months of the year, only to build them back again for the summer. She knew, of course, the natural reasons why it happened, it just seemed out of sync from a human perspective. Perhaps that was what was wrong with the world, the inability of humans to see things from another perspective. To accept that what works for them might not work for all manner of other species, even other humans.

Annie felt the itching of a thought forming in her head. She opened the window a crack and let the air blow across her forehead, ruffling the tufts of hair that always grew soft and out of control there. Peach fuzz she called it, or baby hairs, because it was so soft and completely unmanageable. *Baby hairs?* That was it. That was what had been bugging Annie since Ian had told them he and Nicole didn't have secrets.

"Swift," Annie almost shouted, twisting in her seat to face the DI. "The pills we found in the cream pot in Nicole's room, the ones I thought looked like contraceptive pills, do you remember?"

"Yep," Swift answered. "But can you try to keep your light bulb moments down a notch when I'm driving, I nearly went right into that bramble hedge."

"Says more about your driving," Annie muttered under her breath with a grin.

"I heard that," Swift replied.

"You were meant to. And, more importantly, I'm wondering what's going on with Ian and Nicole. Olivia said they'd gotten married in secret, right?"

"Right." Swift drew the word out as long as he could.

"And Ian wanted them to have a baby, yes?"

"That's what Olivia said, yeah."

"So maybe Nicole was hiding her pills, so Ian didn't know she was still taking them. Why else would she pop them all out of their packet and hide them in an empty cream pot?" Annie put her window back up and flattened down her hair. "And maybe she *was* having an affair with Justin Sloan and needed to keep taking them in case she fell pregnant. And, just maybe, Ian knew this and wanted to get rid of the rival for Nicole's affection. It's the oldest motive in the book. Jealousy."

Swift didn't answer immediately, he tapped at the steering wheel with his forefingers, playing an erratic drum beat. Annie could see the red pin on the Satnav draw ever closer and she itched to know more about Justin Sloan. Who was he? Why was he at Paradise Grove? Why did he tell Dina that he was a surprise for Nicole? Why was he dead? And, perhaps most importantly, where was Nicole now?

"I know you've got your heart set on Ian being the bad guy here, Annie," Swift said, eventually, pulling into the grassy drive of an end terrace of what looked like a row of old council houses. "But he's got an airtight alibi for the time of the murder."

Annie opened her mouth to reply and was beaten to it by Swift's phone. He picked a button on the steering wheel and Tink's voice rang through the car.

"Guv," the DS said without waiting for acknowledgement. "We've had Nicole's phone records back and she called Ian a few minutes after she arrived back in her room on Monday morning. Looks like she sent a picture to him too."

"While she was waiting for the police at the hotel?" Annie asked, thinking of all the missed calls from Ian she'd seen on Nicole's phone. Maybe Nicole had called to tell him what had happened and then been forced to leave her phone behind when the scene was cordoned off.

"Not quite, looks like it was before she even told the hotel staff about the dead body," Tink replied. "And, Guv, we've got a BOLO out on Ian Coles."

"What?" Swift said, sharply. "Why?"

Annie tried not to mould her face into an expression that didn't shout out *I told you so*.

"I did some digging and Ian is up to his neck in business debt. He has bankrupted himself on more than one occasion to get out of a mess. We sent a unit to his address to bring him in for questioning, like you asked," Tink went on. "And he's vanished. His work hasn't seen him for a couple of days either. Post has built up. Seems like no-one has seen him since you guys spoke to him on Tuesday."

"Right. Thanks, Tink. Keep me updated as soon as you know anything." Swift banged his palms against the steering wheel and turned off the engine. "I don't get it, Annie. His alibi checked out, with more than one person and CCTV."

"Let's not overthink this," Annie said, getting out of the car. "Right now, we need to focus on Justin Sloan and try and unravel the secrets he's been keeping, because what we need more than anything is a clue about where Nicole is."

Swift glanced across at Annie over the top of the car bonnet, the engine ticking underneath as it cooled.

"Nicole doesn't need a clue, Annie," he said, softly. "She needs a miracle."

NINETEEN

JUSTIN SLOAN'S ADDRESS DID NOT GIVE UP A MIRACLE. It was locked up tight and giving nothing away at all. Annie cupped her hands around her face and peered in the glass of the front door, trying to see past the darkness of the drawn curtains in all the other ground floor rooms. Swift paced the front garden on the phone to Page, calling in some more information about Mr Sloan's next of kin and contact details.

"He's doing some digging," Swift said, pocketing his phone. "So how about we use the old O'Malley and Swift form of entry and see what we can find here?"

Annie flexed her fingers, grinning.

"Is that a cry for help I hear?" she said, loudly so anyone listening in would catch it.

"I think it might be," Swift replied, theatrically. "Let's see if there are any doors around the back."

As the house was an end terrace, the garden took them all the way around to the back gardens of the row of houses. A low chain fence and neat flower border marked the space between Sloan's garden and the neighbours. All the windows at the back of the house were closed too, their curtains drawn.

"I'd bet Mr Sloan lives here alone," Annie said, trying to see in a crack in the curtain.

"Let's find out, shall we?" Swift said, giving the back door handle a rattle.

The door shook on flimsy hinges, but didn't give. Swift gave it a push with his shoulder and Annie heard the locks cracking in the wood.

"It's the police," Swift shouted out. "We're here to help."

He gave the door another thump with his shoulder and the wood splintered around the lock, shards of dagger shaped wood pieces flew in all directions. Annie ducked, her hands flying up to protect her face and Swift tumbled in through the open door with a yelp.

Taking a moment to feel for any damage, Annie peered out from under her arms to survey the mess. It wasn't too bad, probably fixable with a new door surround. She held a hand out to Swift which he took gratefully, hauling himself up from the kitchen floor where he'd landed.

"Hello?" Annie called into the house. "Is anyone here?"

From the dampness in the air and the stillness of the house, Annie could tell it was empty without having to wait for an answer. It felt like it had been empty for a while, too, a layer of dust had settled upon the surfaces in the small kitchen. It was neat and tidy, other than that. Well loved. A sandwich maker and an air fryer took up most of the work surface, and there were no dirty dishes stacked or leftovers waiting to be cleared away.

"Look at this," Swift shouted from through the internal doorway.

Annie stepped through the kitchen and out into a hallway. From it she could see a door to a small living room and the front door. Swift was bent over, picking up the post with a gloved hand.

"Lots of unopened post?" Annie asked, poking her head into the living room.

"Only a couple of letters." Swift flicked through them. "But they're addressed to a company name."

He held one up for Annie to see. *Sloans Ltd.*

"Yeah," Annie agreed. "Look in here, too. Looks like Justin spent most of his life working."

The living room wasn't a conventional set up with sofas and a television. In front of the window was a desk; large, wooden, like a bankers' desk with drawers on either side; a laptop lay closed on the writing surface and a pile of paperwork was weighted down by a diary. A small filing cabinet was tucked away one side of the fireplace, and an easy chair on the other. The room was sparse, clean, the layer of dust notwithstanding.

"I wonder if the dust gathers quickly out here?" Annie asked, trailing a finger across the top of the desk, it came back white.

"It's combine season," Swift replied. "Everything gets coated when the fields are being turned over.

"So you think Sloan was only away for the short time he was in Paradise Grove, then?" Annie asked, heading back out the room and peering up the stairs. "I'm going up, if that's okay."

"Yep and yep," Swift replied with a thumbs up, his head stuck in one of the pieces of mail.

Annie tread quietly on the stairs; they creaked under her shifting weight, the house coming back to life. At the top of the stairs was a small square landing and two doors. Annie tried one, opening it into a bathroom with an old cast iron bath, as neat as the rest of the house. The other door led to a small bedroom with a bed, wardrobe, and a small console table under the window. The mismatching furniture looked chic with a painted wooden floor and muted runner. The bed was made, and Sloan's clothes must have been in the wardrobe because there was no sign of any on the floor or the console, neither had there been in the bathroom. Whoever Justin Sloan was, he was very tidy.

"Anything?" Swift shouted up the stairs.

Annie closed the doors behind her and headed back down.

"Nothing on first look," she said, as they headed back to the living room office. "How about you?"

"I've put a request to the team to check Companies House for what type of business it is Sloan was in. And look at this." Swift held open the diary, flicking through the pages so Annie could see.

There were addresses listed on most of the pages, days and weeks blocked out by coloured pen, with names and contact numbers in the margins. The diary was laid out in precise writing, almost as though written across a ruler. Annie thought about the tidiness of the house, even back to the neat lines of Sloan's trousers and shirt as he'd lain across Nicole's bed, conforming even after death. He was a stickler for order.

"That's a full-on work diary," Annie noted. "Makes us look like slackers."

"Speak for yourself, O'Malley," Swift jibbed. "My diary looks just like this."

Annie tilted her head. "Your notebook looks like a cat's been let loose with a Sharpie, so I hate to think what your diary looks like."

"Fair," Swift snorted. "I don't actually have a diary. I have a well-ordered brain."

Annie wanted to laugh, but she held it in out of respect for the man whose items they were searching for clues. He was lying in the mortuary waiting for someone to come and claim him as their own, for someone to mourn his death. It didn't feel right for Annie to be finding humour in anything right now. She felt a hard lump of emotion sit heavily at the base of her throat and tried unsuccessfully to swallow it down.

Swift flicked through the pages of the diary to the current month. The first week was blocked out, thick marker pen highlighting a holiday to Mauritius. Swift lifted the page carefully to the week they were in. Paradise Grove was written in at the top of the week, the address in smaller capitals underneath. Three days in total were colour-blocked for the seaside resort, the same amount of time that Nicole and her friends were booked in. And there, at the side, in bottle green ink, was Ian Coles' name and contact number.

Swift looked up at Annie from the pages, but before he could say anything his phone rang out into the quiet room.

"Hi Page," Swift said, putting the diary back where he found it and pulling off a glove to answer. "I'm putting you on speaker phone, Annie's here, what have you got for us?"

Swift tapped his screen and held it out so Annie could hear too.

"Hi guys," Page said, his voice tinny. "Two things. Firstly, Sloans Ltd has been a registered company for the last five years, abridged accounts are available to view, and our man is doing very well for himself. We're talking upwards of five hundred thousand a year."

"Wow," Swift whistled through his teeth. "I'm in the wrong career."

Page cleared his throat, stumbling over his next words. "Well, sir," he said. "You might not be saying that when you find out what he did. Justin Sloan was a sex worker. A gigolo. His website is sleek, private, offering male escort services for a whopping fee."

Annie slipped a pair of gloves from her bag, pulling them over her fingers, she picked up the diary. Finding the current week, Annie dragged her finger down the page to the contact name and number of the booking.

Just as she thought she'd seen written there only moments before, yet making no sense now, was Ian Coles' name and number. Nicole's own boyfriend, or husband if others were to be believed, had hired a male escort for his wife's birthday surprise.

Annie tapped the page with her finger, trying to get the attention of Swift.

"Thanks Page, great work," Swift said, his eyebrows meeting in confusion. "What was the other thing you had to tell us?"

"The BOLO for Coles has given us a hit," Page went on. "His reg plate was picked up on a garage out in North Norfolk."

"When?" Swift asked.

"About two hours ago," Page replied. "And he was heading in the direction of Paradise Grove."

Annie felt a familiar lurch in her belly, the kind she knew came with the moment in a case when all the clues were starting to unravel into individual strands that she could make sense of. At the moment, the main threads of the storyline were still tangled in a great knot, but Ian's thread was there and waiting to be pulled, and Annie thought it could possibly be the one which would set the others free.

Swift thanked the DC and ended the call.

"Come on, Annie," he said, setting the letters down on the desk. "Let's get a SOCO team here, we need to get back to Paradise Grove before Ian does any more harm."

"What about his alibi?" Annie asked, placing the diary back on top of the stack of papers.

"I don't know, O'Malley," Swift replied, leaving the house. Annie followed and watched as Swift pushed the door shut behind him, pressing the wood back across the lock. It looked reasonably untouched from a distance. "But I think you may be right about him."

"Ian Coles?" Annie asked. "I thought you said I was being touchy when I told you how I felt about Ian?"

"I underestimated your spidey sense, Annie, and I'm sorry." Swift looked across at her and gave her a smile. "I should know better, by now."

"Thank you," Annie replied. "And even if Ian does have an alibi, what kind of husband hires his wife an escort for her birthday?"

"Let's go and find out," Swift said, unlocking the car. "And let's just hope we get there before someone else gets hurt."

TWENTY

THE HOTEL WAS STEEPED IN DARKNESS, BOTH THE SUN and the moon were low in opposite fields of the sky, yet neither of them were casting any light. Clouds covered both, and it was only the eerie, soft, orange glow that differentiated the sun from the blue-tinted full moon. Annie stepped up to the front door of Paradise Grove, seeing in finality just how run down it had become. The paint work was peeling away from the handle and the knocker, the wood warped and twisted by years of salt erosion. Swift climbed the steps next to her and, echoing around the old building, Annie could hear the sound of the waves crashing across the beach. She'd checked tide times on the way over and they had a couple of hours before high tide. The ever-present encroaching water kept a hard knot of worry lodged in Annie's chest, and she couldn't help but check the new app she'd downloaded to keep track of it.

Swift pushed the door open and ushered Annie

inside. They needed to make sure everyone was safe, and Swift was going to gather them all in the dining room and keep the small team of uniformed officers on site to protect them until Ian was found. But the hotel was quiet. Too quiet. Annie walked through the hallway to the games room and looked inside, it was empty.

"Hello," Swift shouted, coming up behind her.

"Where is everyone?" Annie asked, a chill invading her body.

They carried on up the corridor, Annie trying to be as quiet as possible, as though if her footsteps were too loud or her voice caught the wind, she'd break whatever tension there was threading through the air. Where was everyone?

"Swift," Annie whispered, stopping in her tracks outside Pamela's office. "What if they're hiding? What if Ian has beaten us to it and they're hiding from him?"

Swift put an arm out and guided Annie behind him, he drew out his phone and swiped through to dial Tink.

"It's ringing out," he said, the phone still to his ear. "Tink, we're back at the hotel, where is everyone? Call me."

Annie felt a certain warmth at Swift's protectiveness, but she wrapped her fingers around the door handle of Pamela's office, nonetheless. Turning it slowly, she pushed the door open and looked inside. Again, the room was empty, dark, and cold. Annie mentally counted out how many people were still left in the hotel; the staff, Pamela, Dina, Gloria, Hans, and the guests, Olivia, Joy, and Shelley. Spencer and Page had travelled back to the station with a PC, which left three uniformed officers in the search team. The search team would still be out looking for Nicole, but that left seven people that the hotel was not giving up.

"This way," Swift whispered. "Stay behind me."

"What if he comes from that direction?" Annie whispered back, biting her lip. The fear of an intruder creeping up behind her was churning around in her stomach and morphing into a bubble of laughter.

"O'Malley!" Swift hissed out into the darkness and Annie clenched her lips together and followed Swift up the unlit corridor to the dining room. "On three. One, two, three."

He burst through the door, Annie on his heels, holding his torch up and scanning the room quickly and efficiently.

"Everybody keep still," he shouted, but even before he'd finished the last word, Annie was in front of him, her eyes passing over the empty space.

"There's no one here," she said, quickly scouting the kitchen for life. "Do you think they're all upstairs?"

"Annie, look." Swift was at the window, his torch back in his pocket.

Annie passed around the tables to the wall of windows overlooking the car park and the gardens to the cliff. Through the gloom, she could make out the low lights of the spa twinkling across the grass.

"Do you think he's got them trapped?" she whispered.

"Let's go and see," Swift replied. "We'll head

across the car park and not through the glass walkway, there's no element of surprise either way, but I think a giant see-through tunnel is just asking for trouble. It's getting dark, the search team should be back here soon too."

A cold gust of salty wind blew across Annie's face as Swift opened the door. She could hear the sea roaring; low and guttural. At least this way, they had the cover of dusk. Swift ducked low and sped across the grass to the spa barn. Annie followed, crouching as low as she could, she cut across the path made by Swift, eyes scanning the car park and the illuminated windows of the spa. They reached the cliff edge and stopped, Swift glanced in the window of the pool area of the spa and coaxed Annie over.

"They're swimming," Swift said, the surprise lifting his voice from a whisper to a shout.

Swimming?

"Don't be ridiculous," Annie said, and shuffled past the windows, her body still low to stay hidden. "They can't be swimming. What about Ian Coles?"

Peering over the window ledge Annie saw the unmistakable head of Pamela as she cut through the water of the pool, powerful and calm. The other staff members were lounging by the side of the water; Dina had her feet dangling over the edge, while Gloria and Hans used the low beds to sit and sip iced water with lemon. Joy and Shelley were in the hot tub, their hair frizzing over the top, as the bubbles splashed out of the sides and hit the tiles below. The office door opened at the far end of the room and Tink appeared, her phone in her hand, just as Swift's phone began to ring out. He answered, reeling off questions to the DS who looked amused through the window.

Annie broke away from the spa, moving back towards the cliff edge and the low fence. Her heart rate was slowing, and she circled her shoulders and tried to eek out the stiffness in her jaw. They were okay, Ian wasn't holding them hostage or threatening them into submission. A wash of shame flew up Annie's neck and she felt her cheeks heat. How stupid had she been, panicking that Ian was already here? But wasn't that what the BOLO had found? Ian at a garage on his way out to the coast. It can't be just a coincidence that he was driving in the direction of Paradise Grove. Something was niggling at her, the way it had been this whole case.

Across the North Sea, Annie saw a flash, it vanished almost as quickly as it arrived, followed closely by the low threatening rumble of thunder.

"Tink said they all went to the spa to relax after what happened with Spencer and then Olivia this morning. Apparently, Olivia warmed up quicker in the steam room than her bath, which makes sense" Swift said, walking up beside Annie and putting his hands on the fence, leaning into his arms. "Storm's on the way."

Annie kept watch across the sea, the tips cresting white all the way from the shore to the horizon. It looked like an oil painting, ominous and uncontrollable.

"I think it's already here," Annie replied, just as

another flash of lightening strobed across the purple clouds.

And then the heavens opened across the horizon. A wash of rain passed over the sea, the drops slicing through the water like a million pins, as the skies darkened. Annie watched the wall of water move across the sea and onto the beach, not running from it, instead waiting as it reached the cliff and started to patter down onto her hair. She lifted her face to the clouds, eyes closed, and let the rain wash over her skin. It was cold, refreshing, and as it grew heavier, the pain of the drops on Annie cheeks made her focus shift from the embarrassment of getting it wrong about Ian to the itch of an idea that had been sitting there below the surface.

"Swift?" Annie brought her head back down and turned to him, realising that he'd been watching her, quietly taking in her moment in the rain. She shook her head, there was no time for that now. "You said Olivia had been warming herself in the steam room?"

"Yeah," Swift replied, his cheeks pinkening in the cold. "Tink said she went straight in there after her bath, she was so cold."

"But that was hours ago. Where is she now? I didn't see her in the spa." Annie looked down over the fence to the beach. The sea was churning, working its way up the sands towards the cliff. "Are there still uniformed officers looking after the hotel?"

Swift shook his head. "Tink didn't say, but they're not prisoners, they are allowed to walk around. The officers are all out looking for Nicole, and another car has been on patrol looking for Ian. They're talking about scaling back the search for Nicole in a few days."

Annie didn't need Swift to spell it out for her; they thought Nicole was dead and the search would soon change from a search and rescue to a recovery. It wasn't hard to see why, with the rough sea outside the hotel, it was unlikely that Nicole would be unscathed if she'd ended up in the icy water. But it didn't feel right to Annie, if she'd drowned her body should have already washed up ashore, somewhere down the coastline.

Something moved in the corner of Annie's vision. She turned and caught sight of a figure down on the beach. She pushed herself upright on the flimsy fence, tapping Swift's hand with hers and drawing his attention to what she'd seen. There, almost hidden behind the spa barn, across the sands towards the fence near Market Harpleigh, someone was running. Not an evening jog, this was flat out sprinting. Annie felt something inside of her shift uncomfortably.

"Who's that?" she said, her voice shaking. "What are they running from?"

Swift was already up and over the fence, landing on the sand bank with a thud. "I don't think they're running *from* anything; I think they're running towards it."

Annie threw herself over the fence and skidded down the sand towards Swift. Together they started to chase across the beach, reminiscent of their morning's pursuit, except the tide was further in now, beating its drum against the outer edge of the cove.

"All units to the Paradise Grove beach," Swift shouted into his phone. "Sighting of Ian Coles heading in the direction of Market Harpleigh. I repeat, all units to Paradise Grove beach."

"Swift," Annie shouted across the sand. "You think that's Ian?"

Swift didn't stop, he didn't look over at Annie. His focus was on the young man sprinting across the sands to the broken section of fencing. Beyond it, the waves crashed against the cliff base. If he wasn't careful, Ian would end up being tossed into the sea and thrown against the cliff like a rag doll. But nothing was slowing him down.

"I can tell it's Ian," Swift shouted. "But look at what he's running towards."

Annie's lungs burned with the effort of sprinting along the beach. Her legs felt like they were weighted down, and the coating of wet sand around her ankles was scratching at her skin like a rasp-file. But she didn't stop. Squeezing her eyes to focus, Annie could see over the waves and through the rain, past the edge of the cove, and around to the beach beyond. The cliff formed a small covered inlet, a cave, and at the mouth of the cave, trapped by the incoming tide was Olivia, her arms waving in distress as Ian hurtled towards her.

TWENTY-ONE

FOR A SECOND, ANNIE FELT AS THOUGH HER LEGS HAD taken root in the sand, like the wooden struts of the groynes. Then Ian let out an almighty roar, loosening her feet.

"What's he doing?" Annie shouted over the crashing of the waves.

"I don't know," Swift shouted back. "But I don't like the look on his face. Quick."

Ian had reached the water's edge and was pounding through the waves, toppling over with the drag of the tide under his feet. It didn't stop him, he scrambled back upright and started towards Olivia again.

"Where is she?" he yelled at the top of his lungs. "What have you done with my wife?"

Olivia waved frantically in Annie's direction. Jumping up and down, the waves threatening to overcome her too.

"Please, help me," she screamed. "He's going to kill me."

"I don't like this, Joe," Annie cried, the sounds of the gulls above her head screaming in unison with Olivia. "We need to get to her."

"The tide, O'Malley." Swift came to an abrupt halt at the gap in the fence.

The water was so high now, it rolled around the metal legs and curled into small whirlpools before dragging itself back out, just to repeat it all over again only seconds later. Annie didn't stop, she ran through the gap in the fence as the tide was drawing away, sand slipped out from under her feet, pulled by the tide. She tumbled forwards, her hands hitting the wet sand, jarring her wrists, and sucking her fingers down as though it was trying to swallow her whole. She cried out, hearing the next wave rumbling up behind her. Swift grabbed at her elbow and pulled her upright just as the water rushed forwards and soaked her up to her knees. The cold took Annie's breath away, shrinking her skin around her shins, closing her throat with its chill. They ran around the fence and up the other side, towards the mouth of the cave.

"Where is Nicole?" Ian shouted again, his words bouncing back and forth against the walls of the cave.

Annie couldn't understand why he was shouting at Olivia, but she could hear the anger in his voice, and from the look on her face, so could Olivia. She looked like a ghost, pale against the black nothingness of the cave, the sea coursing around at her feet.

"Olivia," Annie shouted as the next wave retreated back. "You need to get out of there."

"I *can't*." Olivia was rooted to the spot as Ian made headway towards her, blocking her safe route out to the beach.

"Get lost," Ian shouted at the detectives. "This has nothing to do with you." He turned back to Olivia. "What have you done with my wife?"

"I saved her from you," Olivia screamed back. "You were going to kill her. For what, Ian? For what? For her money?"

"Shut up, you witch, shut up." Ian was gaining ground. "I loved Nicole, I'd never hurt her, but I shouldn't have had to ask for money when I needed it. We were a family; it was *our* money."

"You forced her to get married," Olivia shouted, edging into the cave. "And I overheard you, Ian. I heard what you were planning. You and that man they found in her room. You hired him to have her killed so you could inherit her fortune. You're evil."

"That didn't stop you from sleeping with me, though, did it?" Ian's face was twisted in a grin. "And that man wasn't a hit man, jeez, Liv. I wasn't going to kill Nicole, just catch her cheating on me and divorce her. YOU'RE the one who killed her. YOU. And I will never forgive you for that."

Ian lunged towards Olivia, his hands outstretched. Swift caught up with Annie and put a strong hand on her shoulder.

"I'm coming in," Swift shouted at Ian, over the pounding of the rain on the sand.

A torrent of water rushed off Swift's hair and around his nose, falling from his stubble like a shower. He squeezed Annie's shoulder, an unspoken sign that they were a team and in this together, and then they ran. Using the ebb and flow of the incoming tide, Annie and Swift cut across the sand and towards the mouth of the cave. Annie ran towards Olivia, Swift towards Ian. Swift threw his weight on the back of the man, his arms around his neck. They both fell forward onto the sand and were engulfed in a large wave that pushed them up into the cave. The same wave took out Olivia's feet, toppling her over as Annie reached out a hand. Annie felt Olivia's ice-cold fingers wrap around her own, as her feet were taken out from under her. Both women moved with the force of the water, their hands gripping each other like anchors. Annie felt her chest constrict with the coldness; a grunt pushed out between her lips. She tumbled over with no idea of where she was going until she felt the bed of the cave scrape painfully against her wrists. The water gave them up and spat them out in its belly.

Twisting her body around, Annie sat upright, one hand still holding tightly to Olivia. The walls were coated in liquid green seaweed that moved as though it was still alive, not merely thrown there by the angry ocean. It was hard to see anything past the shivering woman clinging on tightly to her hand, the failing light not reaching into the darkened corners of the cave. But, scanning quickly for Swift, Annie was relieved to see a bundle of bodies at the far end of the cavern, Swift on top of Ian, twisting his arms behind his back. Their outline was soon sucked back into the shadows and all that was left was the rushing of the water as the next wave made its mark.

"Quick, can you get up?" Annie pushed from the sandy floor, feeling the pain through her wrists where she'd fallen.

"Yes," Olivia replied, struggling upright. "I'm not hurt. Just cold. What did Ian mean, *not a hit man?*"

There was no time to answer the woman's question, Annie took her hand again and moved them both further into the cave. The sea retreated as the waves ebbed, though it wasn't going back far enough now to leave the entrance to the cave clear. Another quick scan of the walls, dripping with liquid black water, and Annie's whole world tilted under her feet. She pictured the way the waves had crashed over the tarmac at the front of the hotel, trapping all those who stayed behind. If the water rose that much with each high tide, soon this cave would be completely submerged, and the four of them would be too.

"Where is Nicole?" Ian's voice screamed, bouncing off the walls of the cave. "What did you do with her?"

Annie felt Olivia's fingers squeezing her own so tightly she could feel the bones grind against themselves.

"It's okay," Annie comforted. "Swift has him, he won't let Ian hurt you."

They were right in the depths of the cave, where the curved walls met the gritty sandy floor. Swift and Ian were sitting on a tumble of rocks that crept up the rear wall. Swift had Ian's arms behind his back, the DI's face was hard with exertion. Both men were dripping with water, their clothes stuck to their bodies. Ian looked up at the women as they walked towards him, his eyes narrow, his mouth thin.

"You evil witch," he hissed at Olivia. "What have you done with her? I should never have let you seduce me."

"I didn't mean to hurt Nicole," Olivia sobbed. "She was my best friend. I just wanted to hide her away from you. We came here, after the attack in her room, I thought she'd be safe here, just until the police arrested you for attempted murder. I didn't know the cave would flood. I thought she'd be safe. I even brought her some warm clothes and her phone, left them outside the cave. It was only when they ended up washed on the beach that I knew what had happened."

Ian struggled to free himself, wriggling his shoulders and kicking out with his legs.

"Don't be stupid," Swift said, as he held on tight, the muscles in his neck straining with the effort, until Ian's whole body slumped forwards and he let out an almighty keen.

"I didn't kill anyone," Ian cried out. "I loved Nicole. I just needed the money to buy this place. It was for my future, for my children's future, for *Nicole's* future. I would never have stopped loving her, and we could have patched things up. It was a win, win situation. And I thought if I could catch Nicole with an escort and get that in the papers, I could reduce the price of the hotel too."

"So you were setting her up for divorce, and for your own selfish gain to buy Paradise Grove?" Olivia spat. "You're sick, Ian. No wonder Nicole was so scared of you. She did what she was told for too long, Ian. She lost all her friends because of you. You isolated her. And now she's dead, thinking you tried to kill her."

The hairs on Annie's neck stood to attention as Ian's cries echoed around the small space. Olivia tensed, curling her body into Annie's. The chatter of her teeth made her whole-body tremor and through the dwindling adrenaline, Annie could feel the chill start to creep up on her too. She glanced over her shoulder as the waves pounded the sides of the cave only a few meters from where they were all gathered at the back. Trying to ignore the hammering of her heart in her chest, she let go of Olivia's hand and felt in her pockets for her phone. They needed help. And they needed it fast.

The screen was black and sea water poured from the charging point at the bottom. Squeezing the power button with her thumb, silently praying that it would work, Annie caught Swift's eyes. They were as wide and bright as headlights. He looked back at Annie with a face that could speak a thousand words and Annie felt her own eyes prick with tears as his lips curled into a smile. She wanted time to stop, to give them the space to tell each other what they'd been skirting around for the last year. Another wash of guilt flooded over her for the message from Mim she hadn't yet answered, the calls she'd left unreturned from her mum, all the things she wanted to say to the people who mattered to her, people she cared about. Tink and Page would be waiting for them to return from the beach to complete the small team that worked so well together.

Another rumble came from the mouth of the cave, bringing with it a relentless wave and drawing her eyes away from Joe. The water tumbled over itself, churning up the walls and crashing back down with such force, Annie felt the spray on her face. She waited for it to stop, to begin its retreat back, but this wave wasn't finished with them yet. It kept coming. Pushed on by the force of the walls, the water was trapped and funnelling ferociously towards them.

Beside Annie, Olivia started to sob. Great heaving, racking sobs that moved her whole body. Ian had retreated as far up the rocks as he could, watching the wave come to take them, with eyes so wide they glowed in the darkness.

"I'm so sorry," Olivia sobbed, tears flowing freely. "What have I done? Poor, poor Nicole."

She dropped to her knees, head in her hands, crying out for the friend she had lost, as the water rushed towards her. Annie felt sick, her head swam, she tried her phone again, squeezing the power button, tapping frantically at the screen.

It was no use, her phone was too waterlogged, the

screen stayed black, only her petrified face reflected in the surface stared back at her.

It was dead.

And as the freezing cold wave reached them, pushing Olivia onto her back and taking Annie's feet out from under her, she realised that they were too.

TWENTY-TWO

FOR WHAT FELT LIKE FOREVER, ANNIE TUMBLED OVER herself in the water. The shouts and screams from the others in the cave came in short, sharp, staccato bursts as her head was thrown under the water time and time again. Pinpoints of pain shot through her lungs and her wrists as she struggled against the water, trying to free her face, trying to catch just one more breath. It was no good, the water was too strong, Annie could feel her limbs starting to flail, becoming a deadweight with the cold and the lack of oxygen. Gasping one last time, she felt herself let go and succumb to the movement of the wave. Bashing against something hard, Annie gave a cry, air in her lungs escaping in a flurry of pain. She couldn't hold on any longer, she knew that now and, all of a sudden, it didn't seem terrifying anymore. With a sense of calmness, Annie let free the rest of the breath she'd been holding and prepared herself for what was to come.

Hands around her wrists. It felt like she was being lifted. Annie's whole body jerked upwards, her arms almost dislocating as she was dragged up and out of the water. She clawed in gulps of air, her mouth wide.

"Annie," Swift yelled, pulling her up onto the rock. "Oh god, Annie, are you okay? Speak to me."

Annie couldn't open her eyes, the tiredness was all consuming, her arms and legs were dysfunctional, yet her brain was running away with her.

Speak, Annie. Tell him you're okay. Get up. Find Olivia. Find Ian. Get the hell out of the cave.

She felt a hand on hers, Swift's gentle fingers circling her wrists, turning her hand over in his own. He linked her fingers through his, connecting them, all the while calling her name.

"Please, Annie," he said, his face so close to hers she could feel the drips of sea water landing on her cheeks. "Talk to me."

He ran his thumb across her forefinger, unlooping their hands, then pinched as hard as he could on the skin between her finger and her thumb.

"Ow, christ," she yelled, her faculties returning with a sickening jolt.

She shook her hand free and shot her eyes open, coming face to face with the startling blue of Swift's.

"Oh, thank god," Swift cried, sitting back on his haunches and running a hand through his wet hair.

He looked as though he'd aged ten years in the few seconds she'd been underwater. The memories of Olivia and Ian flashed through her brain like a slide show.

"Are they okay?" she asked, sitting bolt upright, a flash of pain stabbing at her head. "Olivia?"

Ian and Olivia sat huddled together a little further up on the rocks. Ian had his arms around Olivia, kissing her forehead and whispering words to her that Annie couldn't hear over the waves.

The waves.

"Swift," she said, turning back to the mouth of the cave where the water was preparing to flood them once again. "We need to do something."

Swift's eyes darted across her face, taking in her mouth, her hair, her neck, before stopping on her gaze.

"My phone is dead," he said, leaning forwards and tucking a strand of hair behind her ear, his hand lingering by her face. "So's yours. The only way out of this cave is that way, and there's no way we'll be able to swim against the tide."

"But the cave floods," Annie replied, her stomach clenching. "We *can't* stay here."

Swift ran his thumb over her cheek. "Annie, there's something I want to say."

Annie looked at Swift, her brows knotted, her head shaking.

"No," she said, taking in the way Ian and Olivia were comforting each other. "Swift, come on, we need to move."

"I should have said this months ago..."

There was a movement from the very back of the cave. Behind Ian and Olivia. A figure peeled itself from the darkness, clambering over the rocks. As it got closer, Annie saw Nicole, her face gaunt, her hands as green as the seaweed covered walls.

"Ian?" she cried, her teeth chattering. "What... Olivia. What's going on? I thought you were never going to come back and get me. Quick, this way, before it's too late."

"Nicole?" Ian threw himself to his feet, pushing Olivia into the cave wall, but she was quicker, bouncing up and forging her way towards her best friend.

Swift dropped his hand from Annie's face and hauled her to her feet by her elbow.

"Sorry, O'Malley," he said, seeing her shock at the sudden movement. "For everything, I'm sorry."

He flashed her a smile and clambered over the rocks towards the three friends. Ian had his hand clamped tightly around Olivia's upper arm, pushing her away from Nicole and precariously close to the edge of the rocks. The sea gathered in whirlpools under them, and the next wave was already rushing in towards them.

"Ian," Nicole yelled. "Let her go, you idiot. Follow me."

Ian followed Nicole's line of sight to the encroaching wave and dropped Olivia's arm, scrambling up the rocks towards Nicole. Olivia teetered on the edge of the rock, her balance giving way, she cried out, arms circling. Swift was by her side, grabbing at her wrist, narrowly missing being whacked in the face as he took hold of her jacket and pulled her towards him, holding her tightly as they both regained their breath.

Annie clawed her way across the rocks, taking Olivia's free arm and pulling gently. She lifted her head from Swift's shoulder, her eyes red rimmed.

"It's okay," Annie said, glancing again at the rising water. "You're okay, but we need to move, now."

Swift relinquished Olivia and they all clambered up the rocks towards Nicole and Ian. The wave had reached the rocks too, bundling over them as though they weren't even there. Annie felt panic rising in her, and a complete exhaustion waiting to hit. She just had to make it up to the top of the rocks, to where Nicole had ushered Ian out of sight.

"Quickly," Nicole called. "Up here."

There was an overhang in the rock, slick with seaweed and wet with spray. Annie gave Olivia a leg up and Nicole grabbed her hand, pulling her up and onto it. Nicole reached back down for Annie, and she felt herself lifted from around the waist by Swift and thrown forwards onto the rock. She scrambled around on her belly and grabbed out a hand for Swift in return. The sea was at his feet, lifting him up and trying to take him away. He threw himself towards Annie, who grabbed out at him and gripped her fingers around whatever she took hold of, rolling backwards and pulling him in on top of her, the weight of him a comfort in the terror. There wasn't a moment to catch their breath, the water was still foaming up beneath them.

"Up here, quick," Nicole shouted as the water

bubbled under the lip and spewed onto the flat rock they were lying on. "Come on."

Swift rolled off Annie and gave her a hand up. Annie turned to see a gap in the roof of the cave, narrow, hidden from below by the rocks they were standing on. Nicole twisted her head to the side and pushed herself up through the gap, squeezing her shoulders through the tiny space. Annie felt her heart racing as she lifted her hands to the gap and forced her way through. It was small, as though the rock was closing in on her from all sides. The space was so tight, as Annie pushed her body through it, she couldn't expand her rib cage enough to breath. She didn't make the mistake of looking back. Her feet scrambled against thin air before hitting the edge of the cave wall and propelling her upwards. She felt rain on her face, cold wind through her hair, grass under her fingers, and, as Swift's head popped up through the gap in the cliff top, she rolled onto her back and sobbed with relief.

TWENTY-THREE

ANNIE COULDN'T KEEP TRACK OF WHAT HAPPENED NEXT. The static of the police radios, the crackle of the foil blanket wrapped around her shoulders, the warm hands helping her to her feet. It was all happening around her, but she couldn't process it, as though she was the eye of the storm and the tornado carried on regardless.

Five silver bodies were coaxed up the cliff top, towards Paradise Grove, their own foil blankets glimmering in the moonlight. It was only when Swift appeared next to her, walking so close, his blanket brushed against hers, that Annie felt herself settle enough to focus.

"I'm sorry," she said, comforted by the weight of his arm next to hers. "I should never have gone after Olivia. I put you in danger. I put both of us in danger."

They crossed over the dunes, and down onto the driveway of Paradise grove. The sea splashed quietly at the edges of the tarmac, not quite high tide, it seemed impossibly calm compared with the raging water they'd just escaped from. The flashing blue lights of the police cars lit up the facade of the hotel, two uniformed officers marched beside Ian, Nicole, and Olivia as they stumbled up the steps. Behind them, Annie could hear the song of the siren, as the paramedics sped up the driveway before it was cut off by the sea.

"You don't have to apologise," Swift said, stopping at the foot of the steps. "What you did was brave, foolish, yes, but brave. You probably saved Olivia's life."

"But Nicole was there, she'd never have drowned." Annie dug at the gravel with her toe. "I shouldn't have rushed in all gung-ho, I should have surveyed my scene and risk assessed, you know, like normal police officers do."

Swift laughed gently before his chuckles gave way to a rattly sea water cough. "Annie, you're not a police officer." He squeezed out the words as his cough settled. "That's what makes our team work so well. You're... you! And I wasn't talking about saving Olivia from drowning, I was talking about saving her from Ian."

Annie gave Swift a tired smile, all she wanted to do was lie down and shut her eyes. He was right, she was unique, but Annie wasn't sure it was as much of a compliment as Swift was making out. She wasn't a police officer; she'd failed that at the first hurdle.

"Annie," Swift continued, tucking his foil blanket under his arms so he could cup Annie's shoulders with warm hands. He looked like he was freshly out of the shower with a silver towel wrapped around his chest, the sight made Annie grin. "I can tell what's going on in that mind of yours by the look in your eyes right now. Stop pinpointing all the things you think you did wrong. You're not police, and I meant it when I said that's a good thing. You trained in a different way, you're a people person, ugh, I hate that phrase, but you know what I mean. You see what is going on, *really* see it. We'd be lost without you. And if you hadn't gone in to save Olivia, then Ian may never have confessed to setting Nicole up so he could divorce her for a lump sum of money to buy this place. Honestly, Annie, you're tired and knowing you, probably a little bit hangry. Get some food and rest and you'll be back to your sparkling self in no time."

"Now I know you're taking the mick," Annie grinned, and Swift cocked his head and raised his brows.

She wanted to ask Swift what he was going to say back in the cave. But part of Annie didn't want to hear the excuses he had for getting back with his ex-wife and the apologies he was trying to get out of his system as the water had risen towards them.

"Taking the mick, who me?" Swift pulled his blanket back around his shoulders and stood out of the way of the paramedics climbing the steps to the hotel. "Never."

"So Ian was buying this place?" Annie said, her thoughts whirring as her brain defrosted. "His own company is in financial dire straits and he thought this would be the answer to his debts, just as the PR company was going to be the answer to the journalist debts, just as writing for those awful rags was supposed to pay off his family debt. It's never ending isn't it, when you don't take responsibility for your actions?"

"Yep." Swift's lips were still too blue for Annie's liking. She started to usher him up the steps to get him into the warmth of the hotel while he talked. "And he didn't want to ask Nicole for a loan, so he married her in secret and was using this place to set her up to cheat by hiring an escort and a photographer. Divorce was his next step."

"And not only that, he was going to use the escort article he'd commissioned as blackmail to bring the price of Paradise Grove down. What a piece of work." Annie slipped a hand free from the foil blanket and opened the door to the hotel.

"And there's still the unanswered question to our original crime," Swift continued, heading in through the door, and talking back over his shoulder.

"Ah." Annie drew out the word, elongating the vowel. "The uninvited guest."

"Invited by Ian Coles," Swift noted. "Justin Sloan. We still don't know who stabbed him in the chest."

Annie walked them through to the dining room where the paramedics were working on Nicole, a blood pressure gauge around her arm, a thermometer in her mouth. Ian and Olivia were sitting at opposite ends of the room, both clutching steaming mugs of tea. Annie stopped in the doorway, looking back and forth between the three guests.

"I think I know the answer to that one," she said, heading towards the windows that looked out over the carpark.

"Hi, I wondered when you'd be coming to talk to me," said Olivia, sadly, peering up at Annie through her white blonde fringe.

Annie pulled out a chair for Swift and sat down next to him. She could feel the sand rubbing on her skin where it was drying in her clothes. The salt water had shrunk the material and it felt itchy and damp. But that was nothing to how uncomfortable Olivia looked.

"Do you want to tell us what happened?" Annie asked.

Olivia looked down into her drink, studying the murky liquid.

"I feel so awful," she said, eventually. "About it all."

Olivia looked over at Nicole. The missing woman, found again, looked like a child, curled in on herself on the wooden chair. Her hair hung limply around her face; cheekbones poked through her skin. It had only been five days, but Annie wondered if the haunted look was a result of years of manipulation from Ian rather than five days in a cave. Nicole must have felt them all watching her; she looked up and over at them, her eyes landing on Olivia. What little strength she had left in her, evaporated at the sight of her best friend. Annie wasn't sure how much Nicole had heard in the cave, but from the way she dropped her eyes and silently started crying, she guessed it had been enough to know of the betrayal.

"How will I ever make it up to her?" Olivia sniffed.

Annie leant over the table and took her hand. "I don't know if you ever will be able to make it up to her, Olivia," she said, honestly. "But you can be there for her, if she decides that she needs you. And you have sacrificed a lot for Nicole already. Can you tell us about it?"

Olivia slid her hand out from under Annie's and cupped it back around her drink.

"Ian messaged me a few months ago to ask me for help," she began. "He told me him and Nic were having troubles and asked to come over and chat to me about it. I should have said no, right there and then. I didn't even like him as a person, he always seemed too... I don't know, smarmy, too nice. I had very little to do with him when Nic and him got together, to be honest I didn't think he liked me, either. He gave me those looks, you know, like I was talking too loudly, or being too brash. I wasn't going to tone down just because he preferred his women quiet. We got along, but I knew he was badmouthing me to Nic, just like he did with all our other friends. He couldn't get rid of me though, not in the same way he could with the others."

Olivia's eyes flickered shut, she wrinkled her nose in disgust. "He got me out of the way in the end though, didn't he? I bet that was his plan all along. He hated that

Nic had me as a friend, that she had someone to trust and confide in. So he seduced me. God, I'm so stupid."

"You're not stupid." Swift shuffled forward in his chair, lowering his head to try and catch Olivia's eye. "You were manipulated by a man who was used to getting his own way. We're seeing men like Ian a lot now, those who present as wonderful, caring human beings, but who are actually narcissistic sociopaths. Don't blame yourself, he's very clever."

Annie watched Swift as he spoke, calm and gentle.

"But she's my best friend," Olivia said, teary eyed. "I am a horrible person."

She glanced over at Nicole and sighed.

"And Justin Sloan?" Annie prompted, feeling the heavy burden of sleep pull at her. "Can you tell us what happened?"

Olivia bit her lip. "I knew there must be an underlying reason Ian booked this place for Nic's birthday. He always liked to be in control, but there was more to this holiday than just knowing where Nic was. Nic actually wanted to go to Ibiza, but Ian was adamant that we all come here. I started listening in to his conversations, digging. His phone was too secure to hack, but every now and then he'd have conversations that I knew were cryptic. There was nothing obvious in them, but I could tell he was skirting the issue and couldn't talk because I was there. Then, one night as he was leaving mine, I followed him out the door as he answered his phone. He had no idea I was behind him and he was talking about this weekend. When he mentioned payment, and times, and… Nicole's name, I thought he was… I thought the man was here to kill Nic. A hitman."

Olivia dropped her head into her hands and sobbed.

"So you stabbed him to save Nicole's life?" Swift asked.

Olivia took a great shuddering breath and nodded. "I was getting her room prepped for when she'd finished with her massage. We had banners and all sorts. The others were in here having coffee, they had nothing to do with this, it was all me. I had just turned up and he was already there waiting for Nic in the bedroom. I already had the scissors in my hand, borrowed to cut up the ribbon, and I just kind of went for him. I didn't mean to kill him. I just wanted to scare him off. But… when he fell and the blood started pumping out of him, I ran."

"Justin Sloan was a male escort," said Swift, softly. "He had been hired by Ian to seduce Nicole and give Ian, himself, grounds for divorce. He hired a photographer and was going to blackmail Pamela Parris too; that was who dug the hole in the cliff, but Ian already had photographic proof by then. Nicole took a picture of Justin and sent it to Ian in a panic, asking what she should do."

"The twitter photo?" Annie asked. "Ian sold it to the press?"

Swift nodded.

"What's going to happen to me?" Olivia looked like a child; wide eyed and pale.

"You need to get a lawyer," Annie replied. "And

explain everything that you've just told us, to them. They may be able to get you a lesser sentence if you plead guilty to involuntary manslaughter or gross negligent manslaughter."

"O'Malley." Swift's word was laced with warning, Annie wasn't allowed to guide the suspect in the ways that she just had done. He turned to Olivia. "Olivia Grant-Rose, I'm arresting you on suspicion of the unlawful killing of Justin Sloan. You do not have to say anything. But it may harm your defence if you do not mention when questioned something which you later rely on in court. Anything you do say may be given in evidence. Do you understand the charges? An officer will escort you to the car, where you will wait until the tide has ebbed and you'll be taken to the station to be processed."

Olivia sunk into her chair, the tears flowing freely down her cheeks. And in the moment of time between Swift reading Olivia her rights, and the officers coming to take her to the waiting cars, Nicole leapt from her seat and rushed over, wrapping her arms around her best friend.

"I'm so sorry, Liv," she whispered, as Olivia stood from her chair. "I'm so sorry."

Olivia clung on to Nicole, the gravity of what was happening buckling her legs from underneath her. Annie looked away, unable to bear the life changing moment happening between the friends. She felt a hand on her arm, saw Swift as he guided her up from her chair and out of the dining room. From the corner of her eye, Annie saw Ian, a smile on his face, watching as Olivia was taken from the room.

"What will happen to him?" Annie asked Swift as they headed out into the car park.

Swift walked silently across to the gardens, the storm far out over the sea now, the rain pummelling the water in the distance. He opened the spa door and ushered Annie inside.

"He's broken no laws," Swift said, pulling two of the loungers to the side of the pool. "And, unless Nicole wants to press charges for controlling and coercive behaviour then we have nothing to hold him for."

"Jeez," replied Annie, relaxing with the smell of eucalyptus and the gentle muzak. "That's so unfair."

"It is," Swift said. "But people like him will never be happy, you can take that as a consolation prize. Nicole will divorce him and no court in their right mind will award him any of her money, not after what he's admitted to. He'll go on making the same mistakes as before, and he'll never be satisfied. Trust me."

Annie sat down heavily on a lounger and looked back up at Swift. "Always." She smiled.

"I mean, really trust me." As Swift drew breath it hitched in his throat. "Sophia was the same as Ian, always wanting more, more, more. But now our divorce is through, we can both finally move on."

Annie's eyebrows shot up into her hair. The dog hair in the car, the happy-go-lucky DI, they weren't a result of getting back together with his ex-wife, they were the product of divorce.

"Right." She didn't know where to look.

"Sit there," Swift said. "And don't move, our swim stuff is still in my boot. We're going to sample that hot tub before it ends up in the North Sea."

Annie bubbled with laughter and lay her head back, swinging her legs around on the lounger.

"Yes, sir," she said, with a mock salute.

She felt him move away, heard the open and closing of the spa door. She felt her mind trying to mould what Swift had said into something coherent, but as the strands of his words knotted together, sleep took hold and Annie had no choice but to give in to it.

TWENTY-FOUR

A WEEK LATER

ANNIE PACED BACK AND FORTH ACROSS HER OFFICE. She'd tried on three dresses, four pairs of jeans with a nice top, and a two-piece that had gone swiftly to the charity shop pile. The rest remained on the floor in a sad looking heap.

"Urgh," she moaned at the pot plant. "Everything makes me look old and frumpy."

She kicked the pile of clothes and went back to the cabinet to fish out something else.

There were nerves, and then there were *these kind of nerves*. Annie was teetering on feigning an illness and hiding under her duvet on the camp bed all evening scoffing ice-cream and watching re-runs of Schitt's Creek.

Come on, get it together.

Pulling out the rest of her small selection of clothes —living in an office made it hard to hoard—a dress fell onto the hardwood floor and glared up at Annie like an annoyed cat. It was a midi-dress, navy and white striped, classic. Annie had worn it on her trip away with Swift to Yorkshire. Somehow it had ended up scrunched up at the back of her drawer and forgotten about, but it was perfect for the evening.

She grabbed it and ran up the stairs to the tiny shower room on the top floor. Turning the shower up to its highest setting, Annie slipped a hanger through the neck of the dress and hooked it over the rail. She didn't own an iron, there was no room to store it, so steam was her best friend when it came to getting out the creases.

Annie stripped off and jumped under the water, the idea of best friends flitting through her head. Nicole and Olivia had a lot of making up to do, but from the updates Tink and Page had been sending, they'd have the time to do so. Olivia was being charged with Justin Sloan's death, the CPS had more than enough to go on. Annie hoped that the jury would be lenient, but Olivia had stabbed an innocent man in the chest. There was a glimmer of hope in the case that Nicole was bringing against Ian. With the support of her friends, many of whom she'd thought she lost, Nicole had felt able to fight Ian's behaviour. He, of course, was telling everyone he could on social media that Nicole was crazy and had been having mental health issues, but people could see past him. The ones who mattered did, anyway.

Paradise Grove was on its last legs. Pamela Parris had sold for a huge loss to a developer who wanted to turn what was left of the land into a caravan park. It would bring some much-needed life back to the community, but Annie feared there were some locals who would fight them all the way.

Annie blew out a lungful of air, spraying hot water over the wall. She quickly washed and conditioned her hair, wrapping herself in a fluffy towel, she grabbed her newly crease-free dress and headed back down the stairs. She had thirty minutes until the taxi was booked, nothing like leaving it to the last minute, but Annie didn't want to spend too long getting ready or she'd overdo it. And the last thing she wanted was to not look like herself.

HER PHONE BEEPED TWICE AS SHE STEPPED OUT OF THE taxi onto the unfamiliar lanes of a South Norfolk village. The destination had been picked for its neutrality, its isolation, and the shining reviews of its thrice cooked chips. Paying the driver, Annie took her phone out of her bag and smiled as she saw the messages. Rose had quoted a Wordsworth poem about being calm and free. Annie read it as she walked up to the country pub, trying to remember to breath. Rose had a poem for every occasion, and this was no exception. Annie knew she Googled them, but that made the gesture no less considerate.

The night had drawn in, and the soft glow of the pub shone on the pavement. Through the window, Annie could see a small group of people at the bar, others sitting at tables. Her stomach flipped and she felt a wave of nausea slosh around in her empty stomach. Her phone beeped again in her hand. Quickly, before she opened the door to the pub, Annie stole a look at the message. It was Swift. *Be yourself, O'Malley, there's no way she won't love you.* Annie felt her eyes start to water and threw her phone back in her bag before anyone else could poke at her emotions. Taking a deep breath, she pushed open the door and walked inside.

The smell of the thrice-cooked chips was divine, and if Annie wasn't so nervous her stomach had shrunk to an eighth of its normal size, she would have ordered a bowlful before she'd even reached the table. As it was, she glanced around the low-ceilinged room and her gaze fell on a young woman sitting on her own by a bay window. She nursed a glass of white wine, her own attention fixed on something outside, or perhaps a reflection in the glass as the evening drew in. Though her hair was cropped close to her head, the copperness of it, the gentle tilt of her nose, and the emerald of her eyes glinting in the window meant that Annie recognised her from the other side of the room.

Mim turned her head, feeling Annie's gaze, and for a quiet moment the two sisters contemplated each other.

"Annie?" Mim rose from her chair, her limbs lithe, her movements unencumbered by shyness.

"Hello, Mim," Annie replied, not knowing what to do with her hands.

She was the older sister, but right then, Annie felt like she had a head full of cotton wool and weights hanging from her arms. Mim moved across the sticky pub carpet as though it was her own walkway, she gathered Annie up in her arms and drew her into an embrace that Annie had been waiting for, for eighteen years. Mim still smelled the same as Annie remembered. Like a wheat field in the middle of summer, wild strawberries dotting the edge. She shook off the weights and drew her arms around her sister and they stayed like that in the middle of the pub for what felt like an eternity. Yet when Mim pulled away it didn't feel like long enough.

"Come," Mim said, Annie's hand in hers. "Sit down, I've a bottle of wine and two glasses. Are you drinking? Do you drink? Dad always said you liked to steal his vodka from the cupboard, but that was when you were seventeen and… you're not now."

Mim smiled cheekily at Annie, who was blindsided by a memory she'd banked away for so long it felt like someone else's life. Vivid images of blue eyeshadow, high cropped tops, and boot cut jeans flashed across Annie's memory. The wooden cupboard had been in their dining room, cross hatched on the door so the bottles glinted through the wood. Annie hadn't realised anyone knew she was taking the vodka, she thought they had been too distracted by the crying baby. That crying baby was now sitting opposite her, waiting for an answer, bottle of wine poised and ready to pour.

"Yes," Annie said, quickly. "Yes please. I'm a red wine person these days, but I'm happy to have what you're having. Pour away. Thank you."

She knew she was garbling but she couldn't help herself. Mim seemed so serene and at ease with this situation it was throwing Annie all out of sync. When their dad had disappeared and taken Mim with him she'd been just a baby. There were rumours, told to Annie by their mum, that he'd joined a cult, was living off grid, fending for themselves without the luxuries of modern-day life. But this young woman with her perfect posture and gentle demeanour didn't seem to reflect that kind of hard upbringing.

"I'm so glad you reached out," Mim said, handing Annie her glass. Each of her slender fingers was decorated with thin gold bands and her nails were painted the softest of pinks. "I had been waiting patiently since I was old enough to understand what had happened."

Annie tried to process what Mim was saying. "I had no idea where you were, or I would have been in touch sooner."

Annie thought of how her Dad had whipped out a proper family life from under her at the hard age of seventeen. She and her mum had tried their hardest to get over the betrayal, but it hadn't been easy. Their relationship even now was stilted, trust hanging on by a thread.

"If it's okay, can I just check," Mim said, sipping her wine, "that you haven't told Mum about us meeting?"

Annie shook her head. She hadn't wanted to get her mum's hopes up before the actual meeting. "No, no I haven't."

"Good." Mim's shoulders dropped. "Good. I can't let her find me. Not yet. Dad always said it wouldn't be safe."

Mim put down her glass and reached her hands across the table, taking Annie's. Her hands were soft, unblemished.

"He wanted to take you too, you know," Mim went on. "He tried so hard to rescue you, to go back and get you. You can't blame him for you being left behind."

"I don't... I don't understand." Annie took her hands back and gulped at her wine.

"Dad said I was young enough to start again," said Mim, nodding encouragingly at Annie. "But he never stopped talking about you to me. I feel like I grew up with you by my side. Dad loved you, but Mum's hold over you was too strong to break and Dad felt like he'd failed you. He never forgave himself."

"Mum's hold?" Annie felt a trickle of sweat creep down her back. "Mum didn't have a hold. Dad was the one who ran off and abducted you."

Mim gave a bark of laughter, completely void of humour.

"Abducted me? No, Dad saved me." Mim reached her hand over again and squeezed Annie's arm.

"But the newspaper stories, the old wives' tales…"

"Made up by Mum," Mim interrupted, concern etched on her face. "Goodness, Annie, you don't know, do you?"

Annie felt the pit of her stomach run icy cold. "Know what?"

"Mum made out that Dad was the villain," Mim whispered under her breath. "But she was the one to blame, she forced him to leave and take me with him. She killed a man, Annie. Our Mum is a killer."

THANK YOU!

Thank you so much for reading The Uninvited Guest. It's hard for me to put into words how much I appreciate my readers. If you enjoyed The Uninvited Guest, I would greatly appreciate it if you took the time to review on Amazon, Goodreads, or Bookbub.

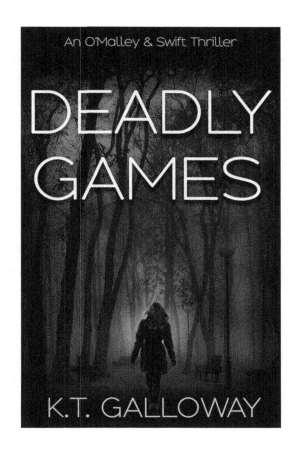

Annie O'Malley & DI Swift return in Deadly Games

THE SIXTH INSTALMENT IN THE BESTSELLING O'MALLEY AND SWIFT CRIME THRILLER SERIES!

Tick, tick, tick... BOOM.

When Annie O'Malley and DI Joe Swift are called to the local park to investigate reports of vandalism, they begin one of the most harrowing cases of their career.

The vandal is a scared young woman with a bomb strapped to her chest and a list of games she must play.

As the games get more gruesome, the young woman has a choice to make; kill or be killed.

O'Malley, Swift, Tink, and Page find themselves racing against time to uncover who is behind the games before the bomb detonates.

But it soon becomes clear that the games-master is a thrill seeker and he's out to have fun, no matter how deadly the consequences.

Perfect for fans of LJ Ross, Alex Smith, Elly Griffiths, and Rachel McLean. O'Malley and Swift return in a thrilling instalment that will keep you hooked from the first page.

SHOP NOW

Printed in Great Britain
by Amazon